Survive!

"The medical student Roberto Canessa was the first
to approach the appalling, yet logical, alternative to
starvation. He talked about it coolly and scientifically,
not pressing but explaining that they were all dying
slowly of malnutrition—lack of protein. There was
little hope of finding the tail section. Even if they
managed to, how long would the food there—if any
—last? Certainly not until late spring when the snow
would begin to melt and they had some hope of
walking out. It was up to them: live or die.
"There were ten bodies frozen in the cemetery.
If they refrained from eating relatives—Parrado's
mother and sister, the Methols' nephew, Francisco
Abal—that left seven. The seven bodies would provide
enough protein to sustain the twenty-six survivors for
at least a month, perhaps longer. By that time, surely,
the snow would have melted . . . And so the decision
was reached."

Survive!

Clay Blair, Jr.

Mayflower

Granada Publishing Limited
Published in 1974 by Mayflower Books Ltd
Frogmore, St Albans, Herts AL2 2NF

First published in the United States of America
by Berkley Publishing Corporation 1973
Copyright © Clay Blair, Jr., 1973
Made and printed in Great Britain by
Cox & Wyman Ltd,
London, Reading and Fakenham

For Fred and Eleanor

CONTENTS

CHAPTER ONE

Cheap Passage to a Wedding

In Montevideo, Uruguay, Hector Mariani, a 54-year-old public accountant, and his wife, Graziela, twelve years his junior, received important news in late September, 1972. Their eldest daughter, Maria, was to be married about October 15.

Had time and circumstance placed such news a dozen years earlier, it would, of course, have been received joyously. The Marianis, then prosperous like most middle-class Uruguayans, would have set afoot large plans for an unforgettable ceremony. Now, times were different. Very different.

A dozen years ago, Uruguay, the smallest of the South American nations, was a kind of pastoral utopia. The land—about the size of North Dakota—is blessed with a temperate climate, where frost is unknown. The soil, enriched by the Rio de la Plata, is ideal for grazing. The early Spanish settlers carved up the land into huge *estancias*—ranches—on which they raised cattle and sheep. Over the decades, the Spaniards and later the Uruguayans grew prosperous by exporting wool, hides and processed beef to Great Britain and the European continent.

Unlike most South American countries, there was no military dictatorship. On the contrary, the prosperous Uruguayans, who had plenty of time to dabble in politics and experiment with governmental organizations, took pride in creating a progressive, entirely democratic and free system of government. Uruguay early instituted what were then considered radical social reforms: the eight-hour day, free medical care, compulsory education, liberal pensions for the ill, the crippled and the aged. In addition, the government, situated in the only large city in Uruguay, Montevideo, hired hundreds of thousands of persons to administer the various social programs, thus bolstering the economy and creating a large middle class. As a result of all this, Uruguay enjoyed the second-highest standard of living in South America, and one of the lowest illiteracy rates.

So long as there was a brisk demand for wool, hides and processed beef, times were good—extremely good. Inevitably, Uruguayans grew lazy. They clung to the easy way of the siesta, instituted by colonial Spanish grandees, closing shops and places of business from noon to three. They sat down to prolonged meals at midday and in the evening, eating a great variety of beef dishes and consuming large quantities of wine. In summer (December, January, February) they flocked to the beaches along the River

Plata from Montevideo to Punta del Este on the Atlantic Ocean, where everybody who could afford it built a cottage.

Beginning in mid-1950, the Uruguayan utopia began to crumble. The development of synthetic materials sharply reduced the need for the principal exports, wool and hides. The neighboring Argentinians, who had swept far ahead of the sleeping Uruguayans in the science of cattle breeding, captured many of the traditional Uruguayan beef outlets. The Uruguayan economy tailspun, bringing on raging inflation and devaluation of the peso. The rich upper crust, who controlled the *estancias* (or related industries), shifted their fortunes from Uruguay to U.S. and Swiss banks, further weakening the economy.

The Uruguayans are a gracious, friendly, warm, fun-loving people who do not like bad news. As a result, they were slow to face the economic reality. Life went on at its leisurely pace. Half the population of three million remained on the active government payroll or on pension. On Friday evenings, everybody still headed for the beaches to soak up the sun and try to forget, leaving Montevideo deserted. By 1971, Uruguay was an economic shambles, with one of the highest inflation rates in the world.

Almost too late, the government cracked down. It imposed wage and price controls, with severe punishment for any violation. To balance imports against exports, it embargoed such luxury items as automobiles, cigarettes, whiskey, fine wines and liquors. Since the Uruguayans refused to do without, a sizable smuggling operation came into being. Corruption spread through many sections of the swollen governmental bureaucracy.

Facing a bleak economic future, the young middle class of Uruguay—especially the university students—organized to protest. They rather romantically named themselves Tupamaros, after an 18th-century Inca chieftain in Peru who rebelled against the Spanish colonialists. At first the Tupamaros merely talked and demonstrated. But then they turned to robbing banks, kidnapping foreign diplomats, fire-bombing foreign industrial establishments and, finally, murder.

The Uruguayan Army, a force of about 11,000 men who had traditionally remained aloof from domestic strife or politics, had hoped that the civil authorities could stamp out the terrorists. When it became clear that this was impossible, the Army moved in, imposing martial law. The soldiers rounded up most of the Tupamaros, sending the leaders to jail. Others fled to exile in Chile, a nation with close ties to Uruguay. Since 1971, the Uruguayan Army, maintaining a low silhouette, has been the power center of Uruguay.

All Uruguayans were shocked and dismayed by this momentous upheaval in their serene way of life. The Marianis especially. Like all Uruguayans, they had watched their pesos drastically shrink in value. Like most middle-class families, their standard of living, once rather elegant, had slipped until it was tough to make ends meet. They curbed all frivolous expenses. In addition, they had a special reason for concern: the oldest daughter, Maria, aligned herself with the Tupamaros. When the Army cracked down, she fled Uruguay to Chile.

For these reasons and others, the news of Maria's forthcoming wedding caused not overwhelming joy but complications in the Mariani household. Maria could not return to Montevideo to be married; she might be picked up by the police, possibly jailed. Thus, if Hector and Graziela were to attend the wedding, they would have to go to Santiago, an expensive enterprise costing perhaps $400, mostly for commercial air fare. Under the circumstances, her brothers, Carlos, 20, and Gustavo, 17, and younger sister Rosaria, 12, would have to remain at home.

There was, Hector knew, one possible way to save a good deal of money on the air fare. The small, 2,000-man Uruguayan Air Force operated a few propeller-driven transports on regularly scheduled flights not only within the borders of Uruguay but also outside the country to Brazil, Argentina and Chile. The

Air Force charged substantially less than commercial airlines. The round trip fare from Montevideo to Santiago for one person was only $38, compared to about $120 via commercial jet.

Hector Mariani went to the Air Force reservation office, called T.A.M.U. (Transportes Aereos Militares Uruguayos—Uruguayan Military Air Transport). The news, he found, was not good. T.A.M.U. flew to Santiago only every other month on the third Wednesday: February, April, June, August, October and December. The plane returned the following day. If the Marianis took T.A.M.U., they would either be restricted to twenty-four hours in Chile or two months, both clearly unacceptable alternatives.

Then, through a friend, Hector heard good news: a group of young boys—some kind of sports team—had chartered a special T.A.M.U. flight to Santiago. This was not unusual. The Air Force regularly chartered planes to sports and civic groups, or to any organization that could afford the tariff. The charters provided extra income for the Air Force, means for training pilots with somebody else paying for the fuel, per diem expenses and depreciation.

The charter in question, Hector learned, would depart Montevideo on Thursday morning, October 12. If he could get seats on the plane, they could fly to Santiago with the team October 12, and return on the regularly scheduled T.A.M.U. flight on October 19. That would give them a week in Santiago, overlapping the wedding date. It was perfect —a cheap passage to a wedding.

Hector hastened back to the T.A.M.U. reservation office. There he found bad news: there was only one seat available. Believing that at least one of them should be present for the wedding, Hector booked the extra seat for his wife. She was delighted. She enjoyed flying; she would be present for the ceremony. When she put out the word to relatives and friends, they responded with wedding presents that would be most useful to Maria and her new husband and easiest for Graziela to carry in her suitcase: money. She did not tell Maria she was coming. It was to be a surprise visit.

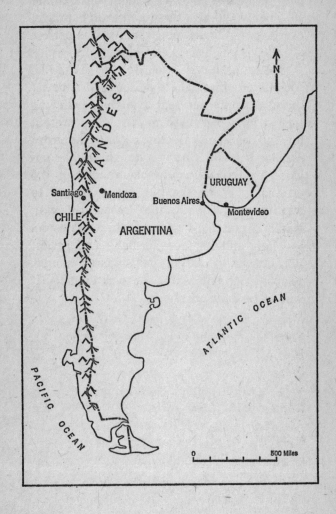

CHAPTER TWO

The Best Team, Technically

Back in the utopian days of 1955, a group of upper-class Montevideo families, most of whom lived in the suburb of Carrasco, banded together to solve a common problem. They were conservative Catholics—ranchers, doctors, lawyers, architects, businessmen— who were dissatisfied with the public school system. They were concerned that their sons were not receiving adequate religious training; that too many traditional values were being swept away by the strong foreign influences touching Uruguay. What Carrasco needed, they believed, was a strict, private Catholic boys' school, patterned along the lines of the Christian Brothers' school in Buenos Aires, 120 miles up the Rio de la Plata.

In time, this group sent a delegation to Buenos Aires with the aim of coaxing the Christian Brothers into opening a school in Carrasco. The Christian Brothers, members of an Irish order founded in 1802 by Edward Rice, received the delegation warmly. After many proposals and counterproposals, the Christian Brothers agreed to open a school in Carrasco. The first classes were held in a temporary building along the beach. For this reason, the school was named Stella Maris— Star of the Sea.

The parents who initiated this ambitious project could not have been more pleased with the outcome. They admired the Brothers, approved of the teaching methods and the curriculum. The Brothers believed that sports were essential for the proper development of the boy into the man. For this reason, the school day was evenly divided between classroom work and sports. In the classroom, English, French (once the second language of the Uruguayan upper class) and religion were required courses. On the playing field, the Brothers stressed rugby.

The game of rugby—from which football as played in the United States evolved—originated in England. Today, each team has fifteen players. Like U.S. football, the aim of the game is to get the ball across the opponent's goal line. A touchdown is good for five points. The field goal is worth two points. There are two forty-minute periods, separated by a ten-minute halftime. Each team is allowed two or three reserves (depending on local rules), which can be substituted only for players who are injured. All others play the full eighty minutes. Rugby players wear special shoes with spikes, but no padding or other protection.

It is, beyond doubt, the most rugged of all

team sports. A dedicated player must keep himself in top physical condition to withstand the brutal tackling and to keep running constantly for two forty-minute periods.

Says a rugby player: "The United States took rugby and turned it into a highly scientific game, with the forward pass, heavy padding and protection, offensive and defensive teams, frequent substitutions. Pure rugby, as played today, remains the rough, deadly game it was in the beginning. You play the full game. You don't go for anybody but the man with the ball. Some men on the field turn into monsters. They kick and gouge and try to whittle down the opposition with injuries and running them out of reserves. Men come off the field with cuts and bruises, broken noses, faces spattered with blood. It is like combat, maybe worse. The men become very close facing such danger and make lifelong friends on the field."

Time passed. Stella Maris outgrew its temporary quarters. The parents launched a fund-raising drive and soon there was money for a substantial permanent building. One of the parents, an architect named Juan Manuel del Castillo, who subsequently died, designed the new building. It was finished in 1961. In later years, the Brothers added more classrooms and a gymnasium. By 1972, Stella Maris was a flourishing operation with an enrollment of 700 boys, all Catholic (or required to convert to Catholicism after being admitted), all carefully screened, all dressed alike in navy blue blazers, grey trousers, white shirts and maroon ties.

There was only one dark note in all this steady forward progress. On May 27, 1969, four former school players were out sailing in a small boat on the Plata River. A storm came up, the boat overturned and three of the four boys drowned: Daniel Costemalle, Eduardo Gelsi and Jose Luis Lombarders. For the mother of Daniel Costemalle, the tragedy was especially hard. Her husband, a lawyer and noted swimmer and water polo player, had recently died, leaving her to care for the two sons, Daniel and Gaston, the younger. After the accident, only Gaston— an excellent rugby player—was left.

The graduates of Stella Maris, those who went on to two years of college prep school, then to the university, missed rugby. In late 1964, the old grads, assisted by the Christian Brothers, organized a team for graduates which they called "Old Christians." They and six other teams around Montevideo then organized a formal league known as the Rugby Union of Uruguay. During the season, they played once a week.

In time, the Old Christians grew into a large organization, a club with about 300 members, including players and supporters. The team itself subdivided into three sections: the A division, B division and Youth division. Each division had about 15 or 20 players. The boys started in the Youth division, then progressed to the B division. Only the toughest and most able made the A division.

As the rugby boomlet progressed, the other six teams in the league subdivided into similar structures. Every Saturday, the B teams of the seven clubs played one another. On Sundays, the Youth divisions played first, then came the main event: the A division contests. The latter games usually had an attendance of about 3,000—girlfriends, parents, friends, other rugby players and, of course, the Christian Brothers.

The Old Christians acquired an unofficial team doctor, an ardent fan named Francisco Nicola, age forty, father of four children. Nicola, a onetime swimming champion, was the son of a doctor who was famous in Montevideo because of a bizarre episode. When one of the senior Nicola's patients died, a relative of the patient went berserk and shot Dr. Nicola. He survived the shooting, but the bullet paralyzed him. He spent the rest of his life in a wheelchair, living on a government pension, dispensing medical advice to all who sought it. The younger Dr. Nicola and his wife, Esther, also 40, were usually on hand for most of the A division games.

The Old Christians gradually evolved into a competent, well-organized team. In 1968 and 1970, they won the Uruguayan championship. In 1971, they lost, but were invited to Santiago, Chile, by the "Old Boys," a team that sprang from the Grange, an exclusive English school. The Old Christians found the Rugby Federation in Chile much older and with many more teams (about 24) than the Union in Uruguay. "Generally," Patricio Campus, president of the Chile Rugby Federation said, "the Old Christians were not a bad team. However, in 1971, the Old Boys were better."

For many of the Old Christians, the trip to Chile in 1971 was an unforgettable experience. To get there, the plane had to cross the towering Andes, an adventure not many of their friends had experienced. In Santiago they were wined and dined in handsome fashion by the Old Boys. Many with liberal leanings were fascinated by the Marxist experiments of Salvador Allende—and became convinced that similar measures would be necessary in Uruguay. All were *muy simpático* with the Chileans, a warm, friendly people like the Uruguayans who shared a common dislike for the aggressive Argentinians who inhabited the country separating them. They drank fine Chilean wines and champagnes. Many were enchanted by the free and easy young girls (called "lolitas") they met in the rock nightclub *Eve*.

Back in Uruguay, the Old Christians faced the year 1972 brimming with confidence. Everybody agreed that, technically, the Old Christians fielded the best team in the Union. The team captain, Marcelo Perez, age 25, son of the deceased architect who had designed Stella Maris, was a student of architecture at the university. Said a teammate and close friend, Oscar Viera, "In my whole life, I have never met a man who carried his responsibilities so well. He was absolutely superb, a born leader and a complete inspiration to every man on the team."

As the year went along, the Old Christians trained hard and played well. But when they got into the finals, a disaster occurred. When they came up against the worst team in the Union, Los Cachila (literally, "shaky old car," a name derived from the many ancient cars on the streets of Montevideo), a team they had already trounced, the Old Christians got overconfident. The members of Los Cachila were "up" for the game. They upset the Old Christians to win the tournament and the Old Christians had to settle for vice champions.

This defeat was humiliating. After the game, many of the Old Christians drowned their sorrows with a strong "cocktail" made of beer, wine and gin. They jumped into a pool with all their clothes on and then, after dressing, took their girlfriends for a wake at a rock nightclub, Zum Zum, or to La Mascota Bar. A few slipped off to the beach at Punta del Este, where a girlfriend of one of the players had a family apartment.

The Old Christians lost the championship, but there was still something to look forward to: the Old Boys in Santiago had issued an invitation for another visit. It fell to the club president, Daniel Juan, to make all the arrangements. He chartered the Air Force plane for about fifteen million pesos ($1,500), then set about trying to fill it up with Old Christians or fans for a round trip cost of $38 apiece, not an easy task. The school year runs from March to November; in October, many boys had to study for important final examinations. Moreover, the news from Chile that year was not favorable: there were reports of strikes and violence, demonstrations for and against Allende. Some fathers did not think it wise for their sons to make the trip in that uneasy atmosphere.

When it was all tallied up, Daniel Juan had recruited 41 people for the trip: sixteen regular members of the A division, including the captain, Marcelo Perez, three other players who could serve as reserves, the team physician Dr. Nicola and his wife, and twenty "supporters." One of the regular members of the team, Roberto Jaugust, age 20, was the son of the director of the KLM airlines office in Montevideo. Since he had a free family pass on KLM, he made plans to go separately by commercial airlines. Daniel Juan excluded himself from the trip. He had just returned from a week in Buenos Aires assisting his sister, who was appearing in a horse show. When he mentioned the Santiago trip to his father, a shipping magnate, the latter did not say yes or no. Daniel interpreted the silence as disapproval and did not press. Another boy, Alfredo Cibils, canceled out at the last minute because he had to study.

The upshot was that there was one extra seat on the chartered flight. It went to the outsider, Graziela Mariani.

CHAPTER THREE

A Festive Gathering at Carrasco

Thursday, October 12, was Columbus Day,
the beginning of a four-day weekend for
many Uruguayans. The day before the
weather had been foul—cold and rainy. But
Thursday dawned clear and sunny with the
promise of good flying weather.

By 7:00 a.m., the small but tidy International
Airport at Carrasco was crowded. The
Old Christian rugby team and supporters began
to arrive by ones, twos and threes,
dressed in jackets and ties, or expensive
sweaters and pullovers. They reported to the
president, Daniel Juan, who had taken his
station by the T.A.M.U. check-in counter.
He had come to see the team off and to make
certain there were no last-minute hitches.

The boys gathered in a festive mood. They
joked—that the plane would surely crash in
the Andes—and laughed and tossed a rugby
ball back and forth. A few parents and girlfriends were on hand to say goodbye, but
outsiders viewing the crowd saw mostly
young, handsome, intelligent, physically fit

boys in their late teens and early twenties preparing for a grand adventure.

* * *

There were five law students—not all graduates of Stella Maris and not all rugby players.

The standout among the law students was Gaston Costemalle, 23, the boy who had lost a brother in the sailing accident in 1969. Costemalle lived alone with his mother, an assistant for the Justice Department, in an apartment overlooking the Plata River in Montevideo. Gaston Costemalle was a brilliant intellectual, active in a liberal political party and a part-time journalist and political essayist. He was an excellent rugby player. The year previous he had been captain of the Old Christians. In 1972, he alternated with Marcelo Perez as captain. He was, of course, a graduate of Stella Maris.

The second was a beginning law student, Antonio Vizintín, 19, son of an auctioneer. Antonio was a graduate of Stella Maris and a member of the A division team. He was a shy introvert, but a tiger on the rugby field. "Vizintín was very different from most of us," a classmate and team member, Oscar Viera, recalled. "Everybody but Vizintín was quite liberal. He was extremely right wing in his political outlook. We kidded him all the time about his views."

The third was a classmate of Costemalle's, Alfredo Delgado, 24, son of a veterinarian. Like Costemalle, Delgado was an intellectual, active in liberal politics. He had a gift for public speaking. He was not a graduate of Stella Maris nor was he a rugby player. He played soccer on one of the university teams, La Loyola. Delgado had never been to Chile. He was looking forward to a first-hand look at the social reform programs of the Marxist president of Chile, Salvador Allende.

The fourth, Numa Turcatti, 24, was the son of a prominent Montevideo lawyer and director of a big bank, La Caja Obrera. Turcatti, who had a twin brother, was a graduate of Sagrado Corazon (Sacred Heart) school for boys and a teammate of Delgado's on La Loyola soccer team. Turcatti and Delgado were very close friends; each day at school they lunched together.

Although Costemalle and Delgado were keen on the trip, Turcatti was not. He was worried about his impending final examinations. At first, he declined the invitation. Later he changed his mind, a servant said, "because he did not want to disappoint his friends."

The fifth law student was Juan Carlos Menéndez, 22, a friend of the others, who had no close connection with Stella Maris or the Old Christians. Although he too faced exams, he decided to make the trip because it was a cheap way to see Chile. Like Costemalle, Juan Carlos had lost his father some years before.

On the evening before the flight, the Turcatti family had a party. Numa Turcatti's older brother had a good camera and took some pictures. Numa then asked if he could borrow the camera for the trip to Chile. The older brother rather reluctantly said yes, provided Numa guarded it with his life. He had heard that in Chile cameras and film were very dear and if not watched carefully might be stolen. Turcatti promised to take good care of the camera. The older brother turned it over with the unfinished roll, including the party pictures, still inside.

* * *

There were four medical students, all graduates of Stella Maris.

The standout among these was Roberto Canessa, 19, son of the noted heart specialist Juan Carlos Canessa. Roberto, just finishing his second year, was an excellent student. He was an outdoorsman, fond of hiking and camping. He played on the A division team and was in such superb physical condition that he had been nicknamed "Muscles." He was also implacably mule-headed. "If you said yes, Muscles said no," a teammate recalled. "If you said no, he said yes." In his medical studies, Roberto had become familiar with human anatomy, nutrition and other specialties of the body. He looked forward to the trip: he had gone the year before and made many friends.

The second was Canessa's best friend and classmate, Fernando Vazquez, 20, son of an electrical engineer. Vazquez was not a rugby player. He was an intellectual, very active in the youth division of a radical political party. During class or study periods, Fernando explored the mystery of life with random jottings and poetry. The latest of his poems was a rather melancholy piece which began: "The road of life is a question without answer. . . ."

When Roberto Canessa proposed that Fernando make the trip to Chile with the team, Fernando was only too happy to accept. But Fernando's father was not happy about it. "I didn't like the idea of Fernando going on an Air Force propeller plane over the Andes," Mr. Vazquez said later. "They don't fly high enough and the pilots are not familiar with flying over mountains."

Fernando paid little heed to these objections. He pointed out that in its entire history, the Air Force had never had a crash on its passenger flights. "What could I say?" Mr. Vazquez went on. "He had a mind of his own. He was an excellent student—received a gold medal for scholastic excellence in prep school. Whenever I questioned his judgment, he would respond: 'Father, what's the matter? Aren't my grades good enough for you? Let me do as I please.' "

On the day before the plane was scheduled to depart, Fernando had lunch with his mother and girlfriend Corina Cooke. He disturbed them with jokes about the plane crashing in the Andes. After lunch, still in a clowning mood, he told Corina that if the plane did crash, he would walk out of the Andes. "All the girls in Montevideo will consider me a great hero," he joshed.

The third medical student was Gustavo Zerbino, 19, friend and classmate of Canessa and Vazquez. Zerbino, one of eight children of a well-known lawyer, played on the A division team. Among the boys, Gustavo was something of a minor hero. In September, 1970, when a band of Tupamaro terrorists bombed the bowling alley in Carrasco, Zerbino had rescued a woman, Hilaria Ibarra Benitez, from the debris.

The fourth medical student was Diego Storm, 20, close friend of the others. Storm, son of an ex-rancher turned investor, was not a rugby player.

* * *

There were three students of economics, all graduates of Stella Maris.

The standout among these was Arturo Nogueira, 21, a player on the A division team. His father was a representative of a Swedish paper company that bought pulp in Uruguay. Arturo was anxious that his family come along—to help fill up the plane. His father declined. He often visited Chile on business and he was too busy to go off on a five-day lark with the Old Christians. Arturo's mother thought differently: she would go. However, a week or so before the flight, Arturo's younger sister came down with hepatitis. His mother canceled her reservation to stay with her daughter.

Arturo persuaded two of his classmates in the school of economics to make the trip. Neither was an athlete.

One was Felipe Maquirriain, 22, son of a wealthy businessman who owned the largest dry-cleaning establishment in Montevideo. Felipe was born in Buenos Aires, when his father worked for Pan American Airways. Later the family moved to Montevideo. The Maquirriains were Methodists. In order to enroll Felipe in Stella Maris, they had to promise that he would convert to Catholicism. Felipe's girlfriend, Mercedes, was also studying economics.

The other was José Algorta, 21, son of an architect. José's mother and father had grown up in Montevideo, where they both came from large families, but in recent years Mr.

Algorta had moved to Buenos Aires to work for a bank as an architectural consultant. José remained in Montevideo to finish school and be with his friends, living with his grandmother. José and Felipe Maquirriain were intimate friends.

On the morning of the flight, Felipe's father, a tall distinguished man with the air of a British squire, got up early to drive the two boys to Carrasco. They picked up José at the home of his uncle, Rodolfo Hareau, then arrived at Carrasco very early. The three had breakfast on the second-floor restaurant, then joined the crowd downstairs at the T.A.M.U. counter. Mr. Maquirriain spoke to the club president, Daniel Juan, then asked a T.A.M.U. official the name of the pilot. "Ferradas," the T.A.M.U. official replied, "the best pilot in the Air Force." Thus reassured, Mr. Maquirriain returned home.

* * *

There were two students who were majoring in mechanical engineering at the University. Both were stars on the A division team of the Old Christians.

The first was Roy Harley, 20, son of a rancher, surveyor and businessman. Young Roy was fascinated with machinery and electronics. He repaired the family cars, radios and record players.

The second was Fernando Parrado, 22, son

of a hardware wholesaler who specialized in nuts and bolts. Parrado was a tall, sinewy boy who wore thick glasses. His teammates considered him to be in better physical condition than anybody on the team. He worked out and practiced rugby relentlessly. He was a car buff, who occasionally entered races. His latest acquisition was a 500cc Suzuki motorcycle.

Parrado had persuaded part of his family to make the trip: his mother, Eugenia, 50 (born in Poland), and his younger sister, Susana, 20. Mrs. Parrado, in turn, had tried very hard to convince her neighbor and good friend, Maria Carmen de Liñares to come along. However, Mrs. Liñares' husband considered the political conditions in Chile too dangerous and forbade her to make the trip.

In the days before the flight, Fernando Parrado had a brief, joking conversation with his good friend and team member, Bobby Jaugust, who was flying commercial on the family pass. Bobby later recalled that Parrado said, "If you get there first, please make certain you have a 'lolita' in every boy's hotel room. If I get there first, I'll do the same."

*   *   *

Reflecting the pastoral nature of Uruguay, almost half of the boys who signed up for the trip were students of agronomy (the science of soil management and the production of field crops), agriculture, dairy farming or were planning to become veterinarians. Most of these were sons of large ranch owners who planned to follow in the footsteps of their grandfathers and fathers, carrying on the family business. Some attended the University in Montevideo, others attended the special school for agriculture and agronomy in Durazno, a small city in the interior of Uruguay about 100 miles north of Montevideo. The students in Durazno commuted regularly to Montevideo on weekends, maintaining close ties with friends, girlfriends and families living in the city, and with Stella Maris and the Old Christians. Among them:

• Carlos Páez, 18, student of agriculture at Durazno. Carlos was the son of Uruguay's most celebrated artist, Carlos Páez Vilaró, a friend of Picasso, Albert Schweitzer, the Nobel-prize-winning writer from Buenos Aires —Jorge Borges, and other celebrities of the art and literary world. His mother, a former South American golfing champion, owned cattle ranches.

Carlos' parents were divorced—the only divorced parents in the group. The father, Vilaró, who had done most of his work in a fantastic house on a cliff near Punta del Este known as Casapueblo, had recently moved north to São Paulo, Brazil, where there were more affluent patrons of the arts. The mother lived in Carrasco, raising two younger daughters. Young Carlos—nicknamed "Memo"—had been pained and torn by the divorce. Lately he had not been doing well in school. He had been losing weight and seemed to his friends to suffer unduly from tension and anxiety. He was not a rugby player, but he had many close friends among the Old Christians.

• Roberto Francois, 20, a student of agriculture at Durazno. His father was a well-known radiologist in Montevideo. Francois was not a rugby player. He and Páez were best of friends and often drove back and forth to Durazno together.

• Gilberto Regules, 21, student of agriculture at Durazno. Gilberto's grandfather had been a ranch owner and a published poet, one of the few in the entire history of Uruguay. Gilberto's father inherited the ranch. Gilberto planned to take up cattle raising when he finished school. In spite of a paunch, Gilberto was an excellent rugby player, who had been on the A division team for three years. He commuted from Durazno to Montevideo in his Land Rover for the matches.

• Rafael Echavarren, 22, a student of dairy farming. Echavarren—not a graduate of Stella Maris—had played rugby for Los Cachila (Shaky Car) and knew many of the Old Christians, including Regules. Rafael was working on the side on his grandfather's ranch near Durazno, installing automatic milking equipment and raising poultry. He was engaged to Anita Lawlor and planned to marry in March, 1973. Rafael was a happy-go-lucky boy, who played the guitar and sang.

• Gustavo Nicolich, 20, son of a prominent architect, who was also a director of the Uruguayan public housing development program. Gustavo, the oldest of four children, was a veterinary student at the university. He was an outgoing boy, well liked by all and intensely active in a liberal political party.

Nicolich, the medical student Diego Storm, the mechanical engineering student Roy Harley, Carlos Páez, Roberto Francois, and Gilberto Regules had been intimate friends since Stella Maris days. They were still inseparable and styled themselves "the gang." The outsider, Rafael Echavarren, had been drawn into the gang. Regules persuaded Echavarren to make the trip, holding out the hope that he might play with the Old Christians as a "reserve."

• Daniel Shaw, 24, son of a lawyer. Shaw, a graduate of Stella Maris and former Old Christian player, had recently completed three years of agriculture school. Afterwards, he went to work on his father's cattle ranch, 150 miles from Montevideo. Rugby was still in his system. Every fortnight he came down to Montevideo to play with an inferior team, Los Cuervos (The Crows), because the training requirements were less stringent.

When Daniel Juan announced plans for the trip to Chile, a friend called Shaw and invited him to go along. The friend held out hope that Shaw might play on the team in place of Oscar Viera, an 18-year-old law student who could not go because he had to study for exams.

Daniel Shaw appeared in his father's home in Montevideo several days before the trip and made his plans known. His father was not elated. The trip, it seemed to him, was a frivolous enterprise for a young man just embarking on a career as a rancher. "I tried to dissuade him," Mr. Shaw said later. "I wasn't too happy about the team going in an Air Force plane. But Daniel was hell-bent to go and at 24, a man in his own right, so my authority went only so far."

• Adolfo Strauch, 24, and his first cousin, Eduardo Strauch, 25. Adolfo was a student of agronomy, Eduardo a senior in the university's school of architecture. Their fathers were brothers who had married sisters, making the boys double first cousins. Mr. Shaw had married a third sister, which made Daniel Shaw, Eduardo and Adolfo all first cousins. The Strauch brothers had been in the jewelry business together. They sold out and bought ranches. The Shaws and Strauches were a close family group, the three cousins intimate friends. Adolfo and Eduardo Strauch were also nephews of the wife of Uruguay's President Juan M. Bordaberry.

• Daniel Fernandez, 26, a student of agronomy. Daniel's father owned a ranch near Montevideo. His mother was a Strauch, making him a cousin to Daniel Shaw, Eduardo and Adolfo Strauch.

• Enrique Platero, 22, son of a farm owner. A graduate of Stella Maris, Enrique played on the A division team, and was specializing in dairy farming in the school of agriculture. Enrique weighed about 200 pounds and was a punishing player on the rugby field. His teammates called him "The Brute" or "The Truck Driver."

• Alejo Hounié, 20, a veterinary student. A graduate of Stella Maris, he was a "brilliant" sportsman—member of the A division team of Old Christians. Alejo was a neighbor of Platero's and a good friend.

• Guido Magri, 23, a student of agronomy. Guido was a former captain of the Old Christians and a crack player. He had a twofold purpose in making the trip: to play rugby and to see his fiancée, Maria de los Angeles Mardones Santander, a Chilean girl who had lived in Montevideo with her family, then returned to her own country. Maria and Guido were planning to be married on December 21. While visiting Santiago, Guido intended to straighten out some legal papers concerning the marriage.

• José Luis Inciarte, 24, a student of agronomy. José's father, a rancher, was deceased. José neither attended Stella Maris nor played for the Old Christians. He was a soccer player. However, he had many friends among the Old Christians and loved Chile. He was planning to be married in April. The trip to Santiago would be his last "fling" before he settled down to a staid domestic life on the family ranch.

• Ramon Sabella, 21, a student of agronomy. Sabella's father owned a farm where he grew fruit—oranges and tangerines. Sabella, called "Moncho," was neither a Stella Maris graduate nor a rugby player. He had been a classmate of Rafael Echavarren in prep school.

Others making the trip:

• Carlos Valeta, 18, graduate of Stella Maris, student in a Montevideo prep school. Carlos was the son of a Montevideo obstetrician. Carlos was not a rugby player.

• Daniel Maspons, 20, graduate of Stella Maris, member of the A division team. Son of a haberdasher, Maspons was a student.

• Alvaro Mangino, 19, student. Alvaro did not attend Stella Maris. However, he played rugby with the Carrasco Polo team and was a friend of many Old Christians, particularly the medical student Gustavo Zerbino. Alvaro had plans to study agriculture when he graduated from prep school.

• Francisco Abal, 21, graduate of Stella Maris and member of the A division team. Abal had given up schooling and gone to work in the family cigarette factory, beginning at the bottom of the ladder. Francisco had played on the Old Christians for six years and was considered to be "great."

• Javier Methol, 36, uncle of Francisco Abal, and his wife, Liliana, 34, mother of four children. Javier, an executive in the Abal family cigarette factory, was known as "El Gato" (The Cat), since he had survived several near-fatal accidents.

• Julio Martínez-Lamas, 24, was a tall, lanky young man with a close-cropped beard. He was a Stella Maris graduate and had played on the A division team and made the trip to Chile in 1971. His teammates called him "Maximiliano." His father, deceased for many years, had been a distinguished lawyer in the Department of Agriculture and writer of essays on political philosophy.

Julio was a clerk in the Central Republic Bank, who processed inquiries from clients. He lived with his widowed mother and a younger sister, age 14. On the day before the trip, his friends in the office made many derisive jokes about the Uruguayan Air Force. Wilton Cabarcos, a clerk, dreamed the night before that Julio's plane fell into the Andes. When he told Julio about his dream, Julio brushed him off with the comment: "I will live many, many years."

• The team captain, Marcelo Perez.

• The team physician, Dr. Nicola, and his wife.

• The lone outsider, Graziela Mariani, bound for a surprise appearance at her daughter's wedding, suitcase jammed with money.

Hector Mariani drove his wife to the airport. When they arrived, she checked in, turning her bag over to the porter. Then they stood apart from the Old Christians and their supporters, watching. They were aware of some confusion: one boy, Eduardo Strauch, had forgotten his I.D. papers. That got straightened out somehow. Then it became clear to them that one of the boys, Gilberto Regules, had not arrived and perhaps would not arrive in time for takeoff set for 8:00.

Upon learning that there might be an extra seat, Hector Mariani made a snap decision: if he could buy the seat, he would make the trip with his wife, even though he had no extra clothing or toilet articles with him. He inquired at the T.A.M.U. desk. However, the answer was a positive no. Gilberto Regules had paid for the seat; he might show up at the last second. Besides that, Air Force red tape prohibited the last-minute selling of no-show seats.

As the clock ticked toward the hour for boarding the plane, the loudspeaker droned again and again: "Gilberto Regules report to T.A.M.U. counter. . . . Gilberto Regules report to T.A.M.U. counter. . . ."

CHAPTER FOUR

Gilberto Regules:
A Series of Curious Coincidences

Gilberto Regules, a key player for the Old Christians, was sound asleep. Why he was asleep is a story that neither he nor any member of the family will ever forget. It is, he said later, "a series of curious coincidences."

The story begins a week or so before the scheduled departure of the Old Christian charter. Until that time, the Regules family had lived in Carrasco, along with most of the Old Christians. Had they remained there, Gilberto would have had many friends and neighbors to make certain that he got up in time to catch the plane. However, the Regules family moved—to a penthouse apartment on the beach at Pocitos, closer to downtown Montevideo.

When Gilberto came down from the country to prepare for the trip to Santiago with "the gang," he found the new apartment a shambles. There was furniture stacked everywhere; only one bed—his mother's—had been set up. Carpenters, painters, decorators were streaming in and out all day long. The telephone had not been connected.

As a result of all this confusion, Gilberto's mother sent him and his father and sister to

sleep at his grandmother's house in a section of Montevideo near the townhouse of
Eduardo and Adolfo Strauch. On the night before the plane was to depart, Regules made arrangements with his friend, Rafael Echavarren, to pick him up the following morning
and take him to the airport. Echavarren, in
turn, made arrangements with his fiancée,
Anita Lawlor, to pick them both up and drive
them to the airport. To facilitate all this,
Echavarren, after having dinner at his father's house, went to his grandmother's house
on the beach near Punta Gorda to sleep.

Uruguayans customarily eat dinner late—
ten or eleven o'clock, sometimes later. That
night, the dinner at Regules' grandmother's
was very late. They were joined by a lady
from Carrasco, a friend of the family. During
the course of the evening, the lady told
Regules there was no need for Echavarren to
come all the way to town to pick him up;
Regules could take her car in the morning,
drive it to her house in Carrasco, leave it,
and have one of the boys in Carrasco pick
him up at her house.

This was a better plan. Regules telephoned
Echavarren and canceled the pickup. Then
he called another member of "the gang," Roberto Francois, and asked if he could pick
him up at the lady friend's house in Carrasco.
That was fine with Francois. He would swing

43

by between 6:30 and 7:00. Regules then called a special service of UTE, the Uruguayan telephone company, and left a wake-up call for 5:30 a.m.

After the long, late dinner, Regules huddled with his father to receive instructions on how to use a camera he intended to take to Chile. "I didn't know a damned thing about it," Regules said later. "I've never taken pictures and I wanted to know what I was doing." The camera, an expensive imported model, was complicated. Regules and his father stayed up until 3:00 a.m. drinking wine and reading the instruction booklet. Finally, Regules collapsed in bed, remembering to set the switch on the downstairs telephone so that it would ring upstairs when the wake-up call came from UTE.

Ordinarily, when Regules' father slept at the grandmother's house, he put his car behind the house and locked the iron gate leading into the driveway. However, this time, he was too sleepy to bother. He left the car out front, the gate wide open, and went to bed.

Two and a half hours later, UTE called. The upstairs telephone, located in the room where Regules' sister was sleeping, rang. Regules' sister answered, got up, and went to Regules' room and woke him up. Regules got out of bed, stood up and looked at himself in the mirror. Then, after his sister left the room, he got back in bed and promptly went back to sleep. "I don't remember one thing about being waked up," Regules said later. "Nothing."

While Regules slept like a log, the clock sped. Roberto Francois swung by the home of the lady in Carrasco where Regules was supposed to be. No Regules; no car. Roberto assumed that Regules had changed plans again, that he was already at the airport. Roberto drove on to the airport. Still no Regules.

Francois, Echavarren and Carlos Páez were mystified. Where was Regules? They found a telephone and called his grandmother's house. A UTE official reported that the telephone was out of order. "Later, we found out why," Regules recalled. "After the wake-up call, something happened to a wire in the switch used to ring the phone upstairs. About a week afterwards, my father took it apart and found the wire just hanging loose. For this reason, the telephone did not ring."

"The gang" was desperate. The hands of the clock were moving inexorably toward takeoff time. Then came the news that Eduardo Strauch had forgotten to bring his I.D. papers. His little brother, Ricardo, who had come to the airport to see him off, volunteered to race home and get them. Francois, knowing that Ricardo must go by Regules' grandmother's house, asked him to stop in and find out what happened to Regules.

Ricardo Strauch set an all-time speed record from Carrasco airport to his home. His mind was fixed on the driving—and returning with the papers for his brother to make the plane. Passing the home of Regules' grandmother, he remembered that he was supposed to check on Regules. He slowed down, looked. He saw the gate open and Regules' father's car parked in front of the house. Since he knew that Regules' father usually put the car behind the house and locked the gate, he assumed that everybody must be up and that either Regules' father had already driven him to the airport or was on the verge of leaving. Ricardo did not stop. He barely made it back to the airport in time for his brother to clear his papers with the authorities and board the airplane.

At 9:00 a.m., Regules woke up. He looked at his wrist watch—and panicked. He had missed the plane! Furious with himself, he dressed, had coffee, then went to Francois' home to ask why someone had not telephoned him. The people at Francois' home laughed in exasperation and said, "We wore our fingers out dialing. There must be something wrong with the phone!"

On the way back to his grandmother's, Regules evolved a plan. He would ask his father for a loan—about $60—to buy a one-way commercial fare to Santiago. He would catch up with the gang in Santiago and return with them in the seat he had already paid for.

Regules found his father in an icy mood. How stupid it had been to pay for a seat on the Air Force plane and then oversleep, he said. Regules conceded that it had been stupid. He could not understand. He knew it had been important to get up. Nothing like that had ever happened before. It would never happen again.

Reluctantly, his father lent him money for a commercial ticket to Santiago.

CHAPTER FIVE

A Fine Plane, a Seemingly Well-qualified Crew

While the passengers were gathering, the Air Force plane that would fly them to Santiago was being made ready at the Air Force section of Carrasco airport, a few hundred yards away from the civilian terminal.

That morning, the Uruguayan Air Force, founded in 1948, listed a total of about 60 airplanes on its register. About half of these were World War II-vintage, propeller-driven T-6 trainers, obtained from the United States, which has maintained friendly relations with Uruguay for decades. In addition, there were 10 single-engine T-33 jet trainers and a half dozen helicopters.

The largest and most viable section of the Uruguayan Air Force was the two transport groups of Brigade Number 1, based at Carrasco airport. One group, number 3, consisted of about 18 ancient DC-3s (or, by military designation, C-47s). The second, Group 4, consisted of four new high-wing monoplanes with turboprop engines. Two of these were Dutch-built Fokker F-27s. Two were U.S.-built Fairchild F-227s, with Rolls Royce engines. The Fokkers had a seating capacity of 43. The Fairchilds, 15 feet longer, had a seating capacity of 48.

The Air Force had selected one of the Fairchilds for the Old Christian charter. It was plane No. 571, delivered in Uruguay on August 13, 1971. It had 792 flying hours and was considered to be in perfect condition. It was, in truth, the best plane the Uruguayan Air Force could provide.

Early on that morning, the crew reported to Brigade Operations. They were five: the plane's captain, Colonel Julio Cesar Ferradas, 39; the second-in-command, Lt. Colonel Dante Hector Lagurara, 41; the navigator, Lieutenant Ramon Martinez, 30; and two enlisted men, the mechanic, Carlos Roque, 24, and a steward, Ovidio Ramirez, 26.

The crew was seemingly well-qualified. The plane commander, Ferradas, one of 155 pilots in the Uruguayan Air Force, had 5,116 flying hours, 552 of them in the new Fairchilds and Fokkers. He had flown one of the Fairchilds from the factory in Hagerstown, Maryland, to Montevideo. In the previous three months, he had flown plane Number 571 for 76 hours. In all, he had made the Montevideo-Santiago flight across the Andes 29 times, a dozen times within the past year. The co-pilot, Lagurara, was an ex-jet fighter pilot and therefore had fewer hours: 1,984. About 505 of his total had been accumulated in the Fokkers and Fairchilds. He had made the Montevideo-Santiago round trip across the Andes ten times. The navigator, Martinez, one of 23 in the Air Force, had been a navigator for nine years, during which he had accumulated 1,200 flying hours. The mechanic, Roque, had been in Group 4 for four years and was a specialist on the Fokkers and Fairchilds.

One of the five crewmen, the co-pilot Lagurara, had narrowly escaped death in an air accident in 1963. While flying formation in a jet fighter with another jet, the two planes collided. Lagurara managed to eject and save himself by parachute. The other pilot was killed. His plane crashed into a house, killing a woman. In the investigation which took place after the accident, Lagurara was exonerated of all blame. It was determined that the pilot who was killed had rammed the tail of Lagurara's plane, causing the accident.

The custom in the transport division of the Uruguayan Air Force is for the less experienced co-pilot to fly the aircraft sitting in the left seat in the cockpit. The plane commander, or pilot, sits in the right seat usually reserved for the co-pilot. In this manner, the less experienced pilots gain experience under the watchful eye of the plane commander. In one sense, every flight of an Uruguayan transport plane is a training flight.

Again, in accordance with training custom, the co-pilot, Lagurara, filed the flight plan at

Operations. By his plan, plane 571 would fly non-stop from Montevideo to Santiago, a distance of about 900 miles, roughly equivalent to a flight from Boston to Chicago, or New York to Jacksonville, Florida. Allowing for prevailing headwinds from the west, the Fairchild, with a cruising speed of 240 knots, was programmed to make the flight in about four hours. The route: Montevideo, Uruguay to Buenos Aires, Argentina to Mendoza, Argentina, to Santiago, Chile.

The first three and a half hours of the flight would be routine; the last thirty minutes not-so-routine. On the last leg, Mendoza to Santiago, the aircraft would have to cross *Los Cordillera* (literally, The Backbone)— the Andes Mountains. The Andes, an awesome range thrown up hundreds of millions of years ago, probably when the floor of the Pacific Ocean collided with the continental shelf of South America, run north and south along the eastern border of Chile. The range, including foothills, is about 90 miles wide. The mountaintops in the center average 14,-000 feet. One peak, Aconcagua, is 22,835 feet, the highest mountain in the Western Hemisphere.

The Fairchild had a flight ceiling, under normal circumstances, of 22,500 feet. (With cabin pressurization turned off, it could reach 25,000 feet.) This limitation meant that it could not fly *over* the Andes like a commer-

cial jet, but had to fly *through* the Andes, in
passes between the mountains. When the
weather was good—that is, visibility good—
and the Fairchild could fly by visual flight
rules (VFR), there were four passes available: Juncal, Nieves, Alvarado or Planchon.
Juncal was the most direct route from Mendoza to Santiago, and the pass most often
used by planes with relatively low altitude
ceilings like the Fairchild.

If the weather was bad—that is, visibility
limited—it was a different story. By international agreement, the Fairchild would have
to fly instrument flight rules (IFR). During
IFR conditions, the minimum ceiling for Juncal Pass was 26,000 feet, too high for the Fairchild. Nieves and Alvarado had no instru-
mentation and were, in effect, closed during
bad weather. The fourth pass, Planchon, the
southernmost of the four, had a minimum
IFR ceiling of 16,000 feet. Thus, if the crew
encountered IFR conditions, the Fairchild
would have to turn south at Mendoza and
cross via Planchon.

Ever since aircraft began flying the Andes
in the 1920s, pilots have treated the range with
extreme respect. The strong prevailing winds
(average 30–40 knots) blowing off the Pacific
Ocean generate severe turbulence when they
whistle into the canyons and gorges of the
Andes. Said one pilot: "The winds get compressed when they go through the canyons

and build up tremendous speed—60 or 70 knots. They wind around the peaks and go back in the direction they came from, colliding with the new, onrushing winds. This forces some winds to go straight up—or straight down. An aircraft caught in that kind of vortex can spin like a leaf, drop like a brick, or rise like a feather."

There is another problem. Many of the taller mountains are covered with glaciers and eternal snow. In the afternoons, when the sun shines brightly on the snow, it reflects off the surface, and the air, heated by the reflection, rises sharply. This rising air may intermingle with the crazy-quilt of the prevailing winds, creating a complete chaos of air currents that sometimes reach 100 knots. "For this reason," an experienced Andes pilot said, "nobody in his right mind will fly low in the Andes after eleven o'clock in the morning."

Over the years, the Andes have claimed many aircraft, some forever lost in the maze of canyons and deep gorges. The most recent loss had occurred the previous July. A four-engine aircraft left Carrasco bound for Santiago, with a load of 86 live cattle to be used for breeding purposes. The plane had a crew of six, including three Uruguayans, one a former member of the Uruguayan Air Force. It crashed in the Andes and was never found.

The most spectacular and bizarre aircraft crash in the Andes occurred in April, 1961.

An LAN-Chile commercial charter was flying a Chilean soccer team, the Green Cross, from the area in the south to Santiago. The plane encountered a storm, iced up and was blown into the Andes. After a long and futile search, LAN-Chile crossed the plane off as forever lost. However, a Santiago parapsychologist—a distinguished lawyer with the government—emerged from a trance with what he claimed to be the exact latitude and longitude of the crash. LAN-Chile was skeptical, but searched the coordinates. They found the plane exactly where the parapsychologist said it would be. It had crashed into a wall of granite and burned, killing the five crewmen and twenty-four men of the Green Cross team, probably on impact.

When Lagurara filed the flight plan for plane Number 571 at Brigade Operations, there was a severe cold front crossing the Andes from the southwest. It had come up from the Antarctic, part of the unfavorable weather system that had been slamming Chile all winter, piling up more snow in the Andes than at any time in the last forty years. (It had even snowed in Santiago, an unheard-of event.) The cold front had touched off chaotic weather conditions in the mountains.

Later, Uruguayan pilot Raul Rodriguez Escalada, who flies for the Uruguayan national airline Pluna and has 22,000 hours at the controls, said: "I don't know whether they checked the weather in the Andes or not. The reports were available to them: every evening at 5:30 Buenos Aires broadcasts weather for the whole area. However, I will say this: if I had been the pilot of the Fairchild and I had seen that a cold front had hit the Andes, I would never have taken off from Carrasco. It was plain stupidity."

CHAPTER SIX

An Unscheduled Evening Promenade

After the search for Gilberto Regules had been abandoned, the T.A.M.U. officials crossed his name off the passenger list and the others filed through the gate to Air Force plane 571 which had been taxied up from Brigade Operations to the civilian terminal at Carrasco. One by one they boarded the plane which was painted stark white and bore the words FUERZA AEREA URUGUAY (Uruguayan Air Force) on the fuselage in black.

The passengers entered the plane by climbing a short ladder to a door on the left front side of the fuselage. The co-pilot, Lagurara, was in the left cockpit seat; Ferradas was in the right. The navigator, Martinez, was not actually serving as navigator but rather as an "administrator" keeping the paperwork. He sat in the rear of the plane near the small galley, briefcase open, official forms spread about. The mechanic, Roque, sat on a small jump seat directly behind the pilot and co-pilot. The steward, Ovidio Ramirez, stood inside the door directing the Old Christians and their supporters to their seats.

The Fairchild had few comforts. Some of the luggage was stored in a section in the tail, but much of it was stored in two bins formed of heavy webbing just inside the door in the forward end of the fuselage. The seats, two abreast on either side of the aisle, were hard by commercial standards. There were no pillows or blankets. Since the flight was to arrive in Santiago at noon, more or less, the plane carried no breakfast or lunch in the galley space. Just coffee, herbs for making *mate* (a mixture of herbs and hot water, not universally popular), a few colas and small sandwich snacks.

When the forty passengers—five women, thirty-five boys and men—had buckled their seatbelts, the steward closed the door. Lagurara revved the Rolls Royce engines and taxied to the takeoff runway. Building power, Lagurara released the brakes. The Fairchild lurched slightly, then began to roll. Lagurara used a lot of runway. Counting all the people and the luggage, the Fairchild was loaded heavily. At 8:02, the wheels lifted off the runway.

The Fairchild lifted steadily, rising above the rich, pastoral landscape surrounding the airport, then over Carrasco, where most of the boys on the plane lived. Those with window seats had a good view and excitedly pointed out landmarks, streets, and then the beach on the Rio de la Plata. Rising higher, the Fairchild flew over Pocitos Beach, then the broad *avenidas* sweeping through downtown Montevideo. It was a beautiful spring day. The sun glinted off the whirling propellers. The "No Fumar" sign went off and those who smoked lit up. When the seatbelt sign was turned off, many boys got up and walked back and forth, visiting.

Within thirty minutes, the Fairchild was over Buenos Aires, a huge and glamorous city compared to Montevideo. The boys pressed against the oval windows for a better look. Some traded seats so that others might look. But Buenos Aires was soon left behind. The Fairchild droned west over the flat, fertile pampas, a great plain stretching west (and south) from Buenos Aires, in effect, a huge prairie where the superior cattle of Argentina graze. To the students of agronomy and agriculture, it was fascinating. To others, it was monotonous.

Three hours passed. Ahead, Lagurara and Ferradas could see the Andes looming up and on the eastern side, just this side of the foothills, the city of Mendoza. The Andes were covered with boiling cumulus clouds, a certain sign of bad weather. Lagurara talked with Mendoza Control. Juncal Pass was IFR only—closed to the Fairchild. Nieves and Alvarado Passes were closed. The only route left for the Fairchild was through Planchon. The weather in Planchon was bad: the cold front had brought storms. It was already 11:00, the hour past which no seasoned pilot would enter the Andes in a low-flying plane. Mendoza Control advised against attempting the crossing.

The situation, by any yardstick, was absurd. The Andes were closed tight, at least for a while. A simple weather check before take-off would have supplied that information, even a telephone call to Mendoza Control. What to do?

There were two options: turn around and return to Montevideo or land at Mendoza and wait for the weather to improve. A return to Montevideo would mean burning another three hours' fuel for naught (no small consideration in the hard-up Uruguayan Air Force) and the possibility of having to forfeit the money received for the charter. A stop in Mendoza would save fuel money and, if the weather improved on the morrow sufficiently to cross the Andes, it would insure that the Air Force received the charter money.

Having weighed the pros and cons, Ferradas made the decision to land in Mendoza. Lagurara circled the city, studying the weather over the Andes, then swung round and touched down. The Fairchild rolled to a stop, Lagurara taxied to the small airport building, Plumerillos. The unexpected arrival of the Fairchild and its forty-five people caused a flap in immigration and customs, but soon all were passed through into Argentina.

Lagurara and Ferradas consulted with officials at the airport about the weather. No one could provide any solid information. With a cold front moving through, they could only guess. Certainly it would not be clear that day . . . perhaps tomorrow. Lagurara and Ferradas briefed the passengers: they would remain overnight and try the next day. There was no certainty they could make it. It would depend more or less on the elements—and God. Everybody should keep in close contact, prepared for an early morning takeoff.

Not everybody was pleased with this news. The stopover meant losing a night in Santiago and missing a Columbus Day party their hosts had arranged. Still, there was really nothing anybody could do. The boys inquired of airport officials about cheap hotels and restaurants—the official rate of exchange did not favor the Uruguayan peso. After a time, they crowded by fours and fives into taxis for the fifteen-minute ride into downtown Mendoza.

For most of the passengers, this was the first visit to Mendoza. They found a clean, quiet city of 350,000 persons, a wine and financial center, where everybody seemed to be affluent. Several hundred years back, shortly after the Spaniards had founded the town, it was destroyed by an earthquake with huge loss of life. When the Spanish rebuilt the city, they laid it out with broad *avenidas* and parks and low-slung buildings. In later years, officials added deep cobblestone-lined ditches between the sidewalks and the street paving to carry off rainwater, which occasionally falls in torrents. In addition, they lined the streets with trees. In sum, Mendoza was a pleasant country city, ideal for an unscheduled evening promenade.

The boys checked into the cheaper hotels and set about exploring the city and the shops. They bought presents to bring to their hosts: wine, chocolate, sweets. During the afternoon and evening, they became friendly with the outsider, Graziela Mariani, and integrated her into the group. She joined one group for dinner, then later, about midnight, telephoned her husband Hector in Montevideo, to report the delay and to say how much she had enjoyed Mendoza and meeting some of the Old Christians.

At least one other person called home from Mendoza: the law student, Numa Turcatti. He reported the delay and his hope that the weather would clear on the following day. Turcatti's older brother got on the telephone and reminded him to take good care of his camera.

* * *

While the Old Christians were sampling Mendoza wines, Gilberto Regules, unaware that the Fairchild was forced to stop in Mendoza, climbed on a commercial jet and flew to Santiago, arriving at Pudaheul International Airport shortly after midnight. There he found chaos. The transport workers had staged a nationwide strike. There was no sign of a taxi.

After two hours, Regules hitched a ride into Santiago, going to the Kent and Emperador Hotels, where the Old Christians were scheduled to stay. There was no sign of them at either hotel. Furthermore both hotels were booked solid, without so much as a closet to rent to Regules, who by now was feeling beat.

Mystified by the nonappearance of the Old Christians, Regules set off to find a room. At the El Conquistador, a brand new, first-class hotel, Regules was told he could have a room—but only a double for which he would have to pay the double rate. This was a blow. Regules was running short of money and already deep in debt to his father for the commercial air fare.

Having settled in El Conquistador, Regules then telephoned Guido Magri's girlfriend, Maria de los Angeles Mardones Santander, whom Regules had known in Montevideo. Where were Magri and the Old Christians? Maria reported that she had not heard directly from Magri but she had been told late that afternoon at the Uruguayan Embassy that the plane had landed in Mendoza due to bad weather and that it was returning to Montevideo on Friday morning.

Regules was stunned. The plane returning to Montevideo! And Regules was stuck in Santiago at a luxury hotel. Moreover, to get back to Montevideo, Regules would have to buy yet another one-way commercial jet ticket. Thinking about how his father would receive this news, Regules said to himself: "You'd better never go home again."

CHAPTER SEVEN

"He Had Lost His Respect
for the Andes"

On Friday morning, October 13, there were at least 45 persons in Mendoza, Argentina, who were vitally concerned about the weather in the Andes. It was still uncertain: the cold front had passed through, but there were raging snowstorms and high winds in the Andes. Juncal was still IFR—closed to the Fairchild. The only hope was that Planchon would clear. Guido Magri called his fiancée, Maria, at the Uruguayan Embassy in Santiago and told her that if they hadn't reached Santiago by noon, the plane would return to Montevideo.

That information, it turned out, was far from correct. Nobody really wanted to return to Montevideo. The Old Christians and their supporters were hell-bent to get to Santiago for the rugby matches and the good times. The plane crew was still reluctant to return to Montevideo; the Air Force would certainly lose the charter money, the crew would look foolish for having embarked on a senseless and expensive round-trip to Mendoza. "The unwritten rule of the charter flight," a U.S. pilot said, "is once you leave the departure point, don't turn back." The goal of the crew was to deliver its passengers to Santiago, make a fast turnaround and get home Friday night to enjoy the weekend.

The weather did not clear immediately in Planchon, but there was reason for hope. Throwing the taboo of not flying in the Andes after 11:00 a.m. to the winds, the pilots, Lagurara and Ferradas, put out the word for everybody to report to the airport at about 12:30. That morning, some of the boys went shopping. Fernando Parrado, in company with his mother and sister, bought a gift for his nephew: a pair of red slippers. Gustavo Nicolich bought some items hard to find in strike-bound Chile: a can of fish, three cans of fish paste, some bars of chocolate and two small bottles of whiskey.

Some followed more serious pursuits. The economic science students, Felipe Maquirriain and José Pedro Algorta, decided to have a look at Mendoza University. They took a taxi to the campus and found the public relations director who gave them a brief tour. The two boys were impressed by the size of the school and its facilities. It was much more elaborate than their own school in Montevideo. Algorta wondered if perhaps some system could be established to exchange information and students between Mendoza and Montevideo. After the tour, the public relations man drove the boys to the airport, arriving at 12:30.

The weather was still in doubt. The public relations man told Maquirriain and Algorta that if they had to stay over yet another day, he would arrange for all the Old Christians to attend a party being given by the Mendoza rugby team at a fashionable suburban restaurant. They exchanged addresses and telephone numbers.

The others arrived at the airport by taxi. Lagurara and Ferradas passed the good news: the weather was clearing in Planchon and the plane would take off at 2:00 p.m. While waiting, some of the boys had lunch on the second-floor restaurant at the airport, where wines and whiskey were on sale. Some of them bought wine to take along as gifts for their hosts in Chile. At about 1:30, the group cleared through customs and immigration and went out to the Fairchild. Numa Turcatti, who had taken some pictures of some of the boys on the tree-lined streets of Mendoza, clicked off another couple of frames with the airplane in the background. The airport director sent a guard out to caution the boys not to smoke near the plane.

The Fairchild, which had been fully refueled at Mendoza, required no ground support equipment to start its engines. In the tail section, it had two very heavy nickel-cadmium 28-volt D.C. batteries, slightly larger than automobile batteries. The electricity from the batteries was used to start up an auxiliary power unit (a small turbine), which in turn generated sufficient power to start the main engines. The main engines had generators that supplied 110-volt A.C. power for operating the aircraft radios and other electronic gear.

Lagurara took off at 2:18—eighteen minutes behind his planned schedule. The route he planned to fly was as follows: Mendoza south to Chilecito and Malargue, west through Planchon Pass to Curico, Chile, north to Santiago (see map). In all, it was about 370 miles—an hour and a half in the Fairchild.

In addition to the compass, altimeter, auto pilot and the usual instruments, Lagurara had two electronic systems to help him navigate. The first was the Automatic Direction Finding system (ADF), and the second was a Very High Frequency Omnidirectional Range (VOR). The Fairchild systems were "redundant"—that is, there were two ADF and two VOR systems, backups in case one failed.

The ADF is an old, and relatively simple, system for aircraft navigation. A ground station sends out a radio signal. The ADF antenna loop in the aircraft picks up the signal and a needle on the instrument panel indicates the bearing of the station from the aircraft. To go from Point A to Point B, the pilot tunes in Point A radio station and (after calculating wind drift) flies halfway to Point B.

At the halfway point, he then tunes in Point B radio station for the remainder of the flight, again calculating wind drift. When he arrives over Point B, and begins to pass it, the needle swings to the left or right "hunting" the station the plane is passing. The rule of thumb is that when the needle "passes the wingtip" (as visualized by the pilot) he reports having arrived at Point B. If he extends the trip to Point C, he repeats the procedure.

The ADF system is far from perfect. It is sensitive to weather. In an electrical storm, it may be completely unreliable. At the halfway point between A and B, the radio signals grow broad and fuzzy and precise course-keeping is difficult. With ADF, the pilot must make his own drift calculations, an inexact science that could lead him to fly a sort of zig-zag pattern.

The second system, VOR, is much more sophisticated. It is not affected by weather or other factors common to ADF. The instrument eliminates the need to calculate wind drift. It has a TO-FROM window display so the pilot does not have to remember whether he is outbound or inbound. The navigation bands permit more exact positioning of the aircraft. It has a dial to set the intended course.

To go from Point A to Point B on VOR, the pilot tunes in and identifies Point A (by Morse Code signals emanating from A), then dials in the course to follow to the halfway point. The window automatically displays "FROM." He maintains precise course by keeping a vertical bar centered in the VOR display. At the halfway point, the pilot tunes in and identifies Point B, then dials in the course to follow. The window display changes, automatically, showing TO instead of FROM. When he arrives over Point B, the indicator in the window switches from TO to FROM, and he reports being over Point B.

After taking off, Lagurara fell under the jurisdiction of Mendoza Control. He turned south on airway Amber 26, setting the VOR dial on 177, the course for the intermediate reporting point, Chilecito, 62 miles distant. The display showed FROM, indicating he was going away from Mendoza on the Mendoza signal.

The cruising speed of the Fairchild was 240 nautical miles an hour. There was a strong headwind, reducing the true air speed to 3 miles per minute. At 2:38, 20 minutes after takeoff, Lagurara reached Chilecito. He may have used his ADF to help take a fix, by setting it on the signal from San Rafael, a city to the southeast of Chilecito.

Over Chilecito, a mandatory reporting point, Lagurara radioed Mendoza Control, giving his position and estimating the next reporting point, Malargue, at 3:06. Now he faced a small problem: Malargue had no

VOR for navigational use. Lagurara therefore switched to ADF equipment, changing
course, slightly, to the west: to 192 degrees.

This leg of the flight took another 34
minutes. The Fairchild arrived over Marlar-
gue at 3:08—two minutes later than estimated, good navigating by any standards.
Lagurara reported to Mendoza Control, then
turned west to course 281, following airway
Green 17 to Curico, Chile.

Ahead lay the mighty Andes and Planchon
Pass. As required by IFR, Lagurara climbed
to a minimum altitude of 16,000 feet. The
cloud tops were lying between 14,000 to
17,000 feet. To get above them, he climbed
another 2,000 feet to 18,000 feet. Except for
a few distant peaks to the north, poking up
through the floor of clouds, Lagurara could
not see the Andes.

Planchon, located on the border between
Chile and Argentina, some 53 miles west of
Malargue, was another mandatory reporting
point. There is no radio station at Planchon.
Since there was a cloud cover beneath the
plane, Lagurara could only estimate when
he reached it. Thirteen minutes after leaving
Malargue, at 3:21, he radioed Santiago Control (which has jurisdiction beginning at
Planchon) that he was over Planchon at
18,000 feet. This position report was probably in error. Lagurara was flying against a

headwind later estimated at about 40 knots. This gave the Fairchild a true air speed of about 200 nautical miles per hour. If Lagurara maintained an indicated cruising speed of 240 knots, he should have reached Planchon after about sixteen minutes of flight, not thirteen.

The broadcast from the Uruguayan Fairchild reporting Planchon was the first received by Santiago Control from the aircraft. Santiago Control responded by telling Lagurara that when he reached Curico, another mandatory reporting point 39 miles west of Planchon, he should turn north on airway Amber 3.

At this point Lagurara was fairly busy. If he followed normal procedure at Planchon, he tuned the VOR to Curico, which broadcasts a continuous VOR signal. He dialed in the course, 283. The window should have indicated TO.

Enter now a mystery that will never be solved. At 3:24, three minutes after reporting Planchon, Lagurara called Santiago and reported that he was over Curico. There is no conceivable way Lagurara could have flown the 39 miles from Planchon to Curico in three minutes. In a 600-mile-an-hour jet, yes. In a 240-mile-an-hour Fairchild, no. It is 93 miles from Malargue to Curico, at least a 30-minute flight in the Fairchild, taking into account the prevailing headwinds. Lagurara had flown only a total of 16 minutes since reporting Malargue.

Any one of several things may have happened. After tuning in the VOR and looking at his watch, Lagurara may have realized that he had misestimated the report at Planchon by three minutes and called to correct it, misstating his position as Curico, not Planchon. Or he may have made a simple mathematical error. He had left Mendoza eighteen minutes behind the scheduled takeoff at 2:00 p.m., and may have calculated his reporting points before takeoff. When he reported being over Curico, he may have mistakenly reverted to his original timetable on which Curico was estimated at 3:24. Or maybe the strong magnetic field of the Andes caused a malfunction in the VOR, making the display window shift from TO to FROM, indicating that the Fairchild had passed over Curico. In the past, this had happened to other planes equipped with VOR. Or the VOR signal from Curico may have been temporarily out of calibration.

Whatever the reason, this much was clear: Lagurara was careless or daydreaming or both. It was a time for careful navigating and alertness, by far the most dangerous leg of the flight. If an engine failed or fire broke out or some other casualty occurred, it behooved him to know his exact position so that he could relay it to Santiago, then take emergency action to reach the nearest landing place. Said the Pluna pilot, Raul Rodriguez: "After only ten crossings, he had lost his respect for the Andes. That can be a fatal error."

Santiago Control received the message from the Fairchild loud and clear. Unfortunately, no one in Santiago Control noticed that only three minutes had elapsed between calls. In fact, it was not the responsibility of Santiago Control to check on navigational reports from aircraft under its supervision. Santiago Control assumed Lagurara was correct when he reported being over Curico and followed through with routine procedure. It ordered the Fairchild to turn north on airway Amber 3 and descend to 10,000 feet. The next reporting point would be Angostura, sixty miles north of Curico. Lagurara estimated that place at 3:40, which would have been about right—*if* he had been over Curico.

The Fairchild turned north, not over Curico, but at about Planchon, or a few miles west. Lagurara was not, as he believed, safely on the west side of the Andes, but rather precisely in the heart of the Andes, flying north, toward higher peaks, which reach to 17,000 feet. All the while, following orders from Santiago, beginning his descent from 18,000 to 10,000 feet. He dialed the new course—004—into the VOR.

Going down, the Fairchild entered the cloud cover. Immediately, it encountered turbulence. About that time, Carlos Páez, son of the painter, asked his friend Rafael Echavarren if he would swap seats so that Páez could get a good view of the Andes. Lagurara turned on the seatbelt sign. The plane steward, Ovidio Ramirez, went up and down the aisle, checking that the belts had been fastened, saying, "I think the plane is going to dance a little."

The plane danced hard. Many of the Old Christians began to worry. Some covered worry with bravado, shouting *"Olé! Olé!"* each time the plane bounced. Some of the boys tossed a rugby ball back and forth. The mechanical engineering student, Roy Harley, kept his nose buried in a comic book.

After Lagurara had turned north, Santiago Control noted air traffic between Curico and Santiago that might cause a problem for the Fairchild. At 3:30 Santiago called Lagurara and asked for his altitude. Lagurara replied that he was at 15,000 feet. He did not report trouble, not even the turbulence.

By that time, Lagurara had followed course 004 from the vicinity of Planchon for six minutes. Since the prevailing wind was from the west, he no longer had headwinds. He made better time: 4 miles per minute true air speed. In all, he had flown about 25 miles. Unknown to him, he was roughly following the northward path of the Rio Perdido (Lost River) heading into a triangle of huge mountains: on the west, a glacier-covered volcano, Tinguiririca, 15,400 feet; to the north, Sosneado, 16,929 feet; and to the south of Sosneado, Risco Plateado, 16,257 feet.

At about 3:31 Lagurara, still descending as ordered by Santiago Control, encountered severe turbulence. In one second, the Fairchild, like an elevator out of control, dropped about 1,000 feet. Lagurara then saw rugged, snow-covered peaks through his windshield where no peaks should be. In the cabin, the passengers, hanging on for dear life, also saw the peaks. One passed beneath the wing so close it seemed to Carlos Páez he could reach out and touch it. He nervously asked someone if it was normal to fly so close to mountain peaks.

By now, Lagurara knew there had been a dreadful mistake. He pushed his throttles forward to full power and pulled the wheel back, hoping to climb out. But it was all in vain. At an altitude of 14,100 feet, the right wing of the Fairchild struck a rocky peak.

At 3:31 Santiago Control again called the Fairchild. There was no answer.

CHAPTER EIGHT

A Ghastly Toboggan

When the right wing of the Fairchild struck the jutting peak, it folded back like a giant cleaver and cut the fuselage in half, just forward of the galley. The whirling propeller blades chewed into the fuselage, then disintegrated. The right wing fell into the deep snow. At about the same time, the left wing and engine broke away. The elevators broke off the tail and fell, but the vertical stabilizer, containing one of the luggage compartments and the two batteries in its lower section, sailed down the mountainside, propelled along by the momentum of flight.

At the moment of impact, the forward progress of the fuselage was severely retarded. Many seats broke loose from their mountings and rammed forward, crushing the people in the seats and those ahead. When the wing sliced the fuselage, it caused an instantaneous "explosive" reduction in cabin pressurization and an outward rush of air. Some of the people in the rear of the plane, with and without seats, were sucked out. Then a split second later some of these, still strapped in seats, were sucked *back* into the broken end of the fuselage by the vortex

created by the forward progress of the fuselage. All felt a rush of cold air; some were
splashed with fuel. The noise was deafening
and terrifying.

In those fearful seconds at least seven
people fell out of the plane. Five dropped
at the point of impact: the navigator, Ramon
Martinez; the steward, Ovidio Ramirez; the
brilliant law student Gaston Costemalle, who
had lost his brother in the sailing accident;
the agronomy student Guido Magri, who was
on the way to see his fiancée, Maria; and the
veterinary student Alejo Hounié. All five
died immediately or shortly after the crash.
The steward had a broken neck. Costemalle
was still strapped in his seat. Four of the
bodies fell in a small circle, the fifth a few
yards downhill.

The other two who were sucked out were
Daniel Shaw and Carlos Valeta. Neither had
fastened his seatbelt. Shaw probably died
instantly. Valeta hit the snow, got up and
started running downhill.

After the wings, engines and tail were
torn off, the Fairchild's fuselage dropped into
deep snow, deaccelerating further. Inside,
the fragment of fuselage, the people and seats
were thrown forward again in one great
heap. The fuselage buried itself in the snow
but continued ploughing downhill like a
ghastly toboggan. The hillside was almost
vertical: an 80-degree slope. The fuselage

dug a deep, wide trough in the snow, throwing up an enormous "rooster-tail." On the way down, it smashed against rocks. The nose collapsed like an accordion. The plane commander, Colonel Ferradas, sitting in the right seat, was killed instantly, his body wedged in by the collapsing instrument panel and wheel. The co-pilot, Lagurara, sitting in the left seat, was crushed by his wheel, which was forced into his chest.

The fuselage traveled 6,500 feet (1.2 miles) before it stopped. It came to rest at a place where the mountainside was not so steep. It had rolled over on the right side at an angle of 45 degrees. Although the altimeter indicated 7,000 feet, the fuselage was at 12,000 feet. The tail section sailed another 4,800 feet (.9 mile) downhill from the fuselage.

Toward the end of the long slide, several boys were thrown from the plane. One was Daniel Fernandez. When the plane hit the peak, he grabbed the seat in front of him and closed his eyes. When he opened his eyes, he found himself in the snow, not far from the fuselage, still strapped to his seat. Nearby, he saw his cousin Adolfo Strauch, sinking in the snow. Daniel unbuckled his seatbelt, grabbed Adolfo and stumbled and floundered through the soft snow toward the plane.

The scene inside the fuselage was a horrifying shambles. When it came to a stop, canted to the right at 45 degrees, right windows buried deep in the snow, the people and seats were thrown to the right and forward in a bloody crush. The long slide set off avalanches of snow. They rushed down the mountainside with the fuselage; some snow poured into the gaping hole in the rear. The fuselage was three-quarters buried.

The sudden transformation from comfortable flight to the nightmare of noise and death and cold threw everybody left alive into shock. The few who could think clearly at all had the identical impulse: get out of the fuselage before it exploded and burned (they did not know the fuel tanks were in the wings) or sank out of sight in the soft snow.

Roberto Francois, unhurt but dazed, disentangled himself from the heap of dead and injured and crawled out of a hole into the snow. He lit a cigarette. Moments later, he was joined by Carlos Páez, also unhurt. Then came the medical student Gustavo Zerbino in shirtsleeves.

In that instant, the boys noticed a movement on the mountainside, uphill from the fuselage. They saw Carlos Valeta, who had been sucked from the plane, yelling and waving. He appeared to be injured. He was weaving downhill in the trough left by the fuselage, falling, getting up, falling again. Then suddenly he dropped from sight. He had fallen into a soft spot in the snow. Páez and

Francois set off to try to rescue him, but they sank up to their hips in snow and had to give up. Valeta died where he fell.

The law student Antonio Vizintín was thrown from his seat to the floor of the plane. He felt somebody beneath him breathing hard. Vizintín tried to speak, but no words would come. He staggered out of the plane, followed by the mechanical engineering student Roy Harley and Gustavo Nicolich, the veterinary student. Vizintín had bad cuts in his left arm and lost consciousness.

Roberto Canessa, the medical student caught in the same jumble, had difficulty at first making his mind work. He saw that his fellow medical student, classmate and good friend Fernando Vazquez, the boy who wrote poetry, was badly injured. Forcing words, Canessa asked Vazquez if he was all right. Vazquez replied "No." Then he died.

The mechanical engineering student Fernando Parrado was conscious but had a bad head injury. His head was covered with blood. He had but one thought: get his sister and mother out of the fuselage. Helped by Canessa, Parrado pushed seats aside, unbuckled seatbelts, until he found his mother and sister. Both women were badly injured; they had many broken bones and were covered with blood.

The boys found that every effort, however small, required enormous exertion. The air at 12,000 feet is thin, with little oxygen. At that altitude, many people are not able to remain conscious without oxygen masks. None of these Uruguayans had had experience in extremely high altitudes. They had to breathe hard to fight off the sensation they were suffocating. Fernando Parrado collapsed. Canessa thought he was dead.

The boys who were uninjured, including the other two medical students Diego Storm and Gustavo Zerbino, returned to the fuselage to help drag out the injured. Carlos Páez remembered Dr. Nicola and shouted his name again and again. But Dr. Nicola and his wife, Esther, had been killed in the downhill slide.

Canessa and Zerbino found "The Brute," Enrique Platero, with an aluminum rod (probably part of a seat) rammed into his lower abdomen. Zerbina pulled the rod out. Platero's intestines came out with the rod. Canessa pushed them back in, then hastily closed the wound, binding it with a piece of cloth. They found Rafael Echavarren with his right calf badly mauled, muscles hanging out. They banadaged it with the lining of Carlos Páez's sportcoat, an expensive garment bought in Paris. Up in the cockpit, they found the co-pilot, Lagurara, in terrible pain, his chest crushed by the wheel. There was not much they could do to help him. Lagurara pleaded with the boys to find his suitcase and bring him his pistol so he could kill himself. They could not find the pistol.

In his delirium, Lagurara cried out again and again: "We passed Curico . . . we passed Curico. . . ." This incorrect information was all the boys got from the crew about their probable position. They believed it because Lagurara was the pilot. The mechanic, Carlos Roque, the only member of the crew who survived the crash, was no help. He had suffered a head wound and shock and walked about like a zombie.

For the few who remembered anything about these first few hours, it all was a horrible, exhausting nightmare. Most remembered nothing at all, or would not let themselves remember. When it was clear the plane would not burn, or sink forever in the snow, those who were able separated the dead from the badly injured and the lightly injured. They dragged the injured back into the fuselage; those they expected to die were left in the snow unconscious and bleeding. Fernando Parrado was left outside.

When the plane crashed, the sun passed behind the western peaks, behind the clouds through which the plane had descended. An hour or so later, it began to get dark and snow flurries fell, covering the plane and the blood-soaked bodies outside. The temperature dropped steadily, down to well below zero. The boys dug into the luggage in the forward compartment, getting sweaters, blazers, dry shoes and socks, extra shirts.

The struggle was now to keep from freezing to death. The survivors and the injured huddled together in the forward cabin like a nest of snakes. They rubbed one another's arms and legs to keep the circulation going and breathed on each other. Roberto Francois lay atop Parrado's mother. Her last warmth helped Francois endure the night. Canessa believed that some of the injured—those who were unable to stir—were suffocated in the heap.

Many bottles of wine which the boys had bought in Mendoza survived the crash unbroken. Some of the boys passed these around. At that altitude, the alcohol, combined with the cold and shock, was strong. Carlos Páez, for example, passed out. He and others welcomed the sleep, the temporary escape from the horrible reality. Many did not sleep and many were irrational. One boy kept repeating again and again that he was the President of Uruguay. Another said he was going down the hill to a bar and get a coke. Many cried. Canessa told them to "shut up."

And so, the Old Christians and their supporters spent Friday night, October 13, not at Eve's in Santiago with their lolitas as planned, dancing to hard rock music and going off in fast cars, but in a desolate corner of the Andes, fighting for life, trying to shut out the sounds of the dying, wondering what additional horrors lay ahead.

CHAPTER NINE

Hopes Raised—Hopes Dashed

When Santiago Control failed to receive a reply to its 3:31 p.m. call to the Fairchild, the operator called again—and again. Assuming at first that the Fairchild may have had a temporary radio malfunction, Santiago Control waited for the Fairchild to report over Angostura at 3:40. There was no report at Angostura. Nor did the Fairchild appear on Santiago Control radar when it should have. It was clear, then, that something had happened to the plane. It had disappeared.

At 4:30, one hour after the last transmission from the Fairchild, Santiago Control flashed an alert to the duty officer at Servicio Aereo de Rescate—Air Search and Rescue Service, known as SAR.

SAR, a branch of the Chilean Air Force founded in 1954, has primary responsibility for searching for lost aircraft. When it receives an alert, it has authority to call upon the Chilean Air Force, the police, commercial air lines and private aviation clubs for help. The search activities are coordinated from SAR headquarters located on the second floor of the administration building at Los Cerrillos, a domestic airport just outside Santiago.

The SAR pilots are specialists in rescuing airmen lost in the Andes. One of the most spectacular rescues occurred in 1960. A Cessna 172 became lost in Ramadas Pass and crashed in soft snow. The airmen were only slightly injured. SAR could not find the plane, but requested the *vaquianos* (mountain men) of the area to keep an eye out. A *vaquiano* spotted the plane; SAR sent helicopters. Because of the high altitude, the rescue was difficult but successful. The airmen had lived in the plane for eight days.

Over the years, SAR extended its activities beyond searching for lost aircraft. Chile is a country often rocked by natural disasters: floods and earthquakes. SAR has assisted in many earthquake rescue missions, including some in Peru, to the north of Chile. Since its creation, SAR, utilizing some 1,123 aircraft in 2,800 hours of missions, has found and rescued 1,767 people and recovered 621 bodies.

When the alert reached headquarters, SAR commander Major Juan Ivanovic, a bomber pilot with 3,500 hours' flying time, immediately launched search aircraft from Los Cerillos. The first plane was airborne at 5:30, one hour after Ivanovic received the alert from Santiago Control, two hours after the Fairchild crashed. Two other aircraft followed in half an hour. A fourth was airborne by 6:56.

These first four search planes flew a total of five hours and 27 minutes—until it was too dark to see anything. They first searched along what was believed to be the flight plan of the Fairchild: Curico to Santiago. Then, in accordance with SAR procedures, they broadened the search to ten miles on either side of the supposed flight plan. They, of course, found no sign of the plane.

* * *

All this while, Gilberto Regules was sweating out the arrival of his friends. Friday morning there was uncertainty, intensified by Magri's call to Maria. But at about one o'clock in the afternoon, Regules telephoned the Pudahuel International Airport and learned that the Fairchild had left Mendoza for Santiago and would arrive at about 2:30, Santiago time.

Regules and Maria contacted the rugby hosts, the Old Boys. Two of the players and their girlfriends came by, and the six young people went to Pudahuel to greet the Old Christians. Regules and Maria went out on the terrace to wait. Two-thirty came and went. No Fairchild. Thereafter, every fifteen minutes or so, Regules went off to inquire about the Fairchild. Nobody seemed to know anything.

Time dragged on. And on. At about 5:00 p.m., the Uruguayan chargé d'affaires, Cesar

Charlone, accompanied by his wife, arrived at the airport. Maria and Gilberto saw them hurrying up to the airport control tower. When they came back down, Regules could see by the expression in their eyes that something bad had happened. He thought: *The Fairchild has crashed.*

Charlone and his wife led Regules to the privacy of the terrace to deliver the bad news. "The plane has disappeared," Charlone said. Regules, stunned, could not speak. He kicked the bars of the terrace railing. In one fell swoop, he had lost every close friend he had: "The Gang," plus Platero, Canessa, Parrado—all his teammates. It was unimaginable, unthinkable.

Regules and Maria left for the Uruguayan Embassy.

* * *

The news that the Fairchild had disappeared reached Montevideo newspaper, television and radio offices shortly after 6:00. For Uruguay it was a big story. The radio and television stations interrupted regular programs with bulletins stating that a Uruguayan Air Force plane had "disappeared" in the Andes. There were no other details as yet.

At first, most of the parents, relatives and friends of the Old Christians were not unduly upset by the news. Almost all assumed that the Fairchild had reached Santiago nonstop on Thursday and that it had "disappeared" on the way *back* from Santiago with only the crew on board. Only two families had received telephone calls from Mendoza: Numa Turcatti's and Graziela Mariani's.

Hector Mariani, of course, knew the plane had stopped overnight and did not leave Mendoza until Friday. In fact, he was very well informed. He had called the T.A.M.U. office several times during the day and knew exactly when the Fairchild left Mendoza.

He received the news that the plane had disappeared about 7:00 p.m., on his automobile radio. In the first instant, he believed it had crashed and that his wife had been killed. The shock of the news made him dizzy. He turned his car to go to the home of a friend with whom he might share his grief. Then he thought about his children— they would have heard the news—and he drove home to be with them.

For several hours following, there was great confusion in the news reports. The parents began to worry and to gather at one another's homes, or to call back and forth. Then they began calling the Uruguayan Embassy in Santiago.

* * *

On Friday afternoon, Bobby Jaugust, flying commercial on the family KLM pass, arrived in Santiago. Like Regules, he found himself in the midst of the transportation strike and could not find a taxi. Following in the footsteps of Regules, he hitched a ride into town and went to the Hotel Kent. There was no sign of the Old Christians. Bobby then went to the Hotel El Emperador. No Old Christians.

Somewhat mystified—as Regules had been the day previous—Bobby then went back to the Hotel Kent. By coincidence, as he walked up to the desk, there was a long-distance call from Montevideo for any Old Christian. Bobby took the call. It was Felipe Maquirriain's father. The call was brief and confused. Maquirriain, believing that Bobby had been on the Fairchild and that it had arrived safely, hung up before Bobby could explain that he had come by commercial airline. The phone call reassured Mr. Maquirriain, but it upset Bobby. It was his first clue that something had happened to the plane and his friends.

Bobby walked to the Uruguayan Embassy, worried and uncertain. The first person he saw there was Gilberto Regules. Assuming that Regules had come on the Fairchild, Bobby said, "Ah, thank God, you're safe. The Fairchild has arrived!"

No, Regules explained, recounting his story, the plane had *not* arrived. It had disappeared en route from Mendoza, where it had stopped overnight. There was no question about it, Regules went on. He had been at the airport. The Old Christians were lost somewhere in the Andes.

Bobby was stunned.

The embassy was a madhouse. Dozens of calls from families and the press in Montevideo were backed up, waiting. The chargé d'affaires, Cesar Charlone, was on the telephone so long his hands cramped shut and he could not move his fingers.

* * *

Later that night in Montevideo, there was more confusion. Magri's fiancée, Maria, telephoned the Magri home in Montevideo. It was a bad connection and by then the Magris were nearly hysterical. Maria conveyed the news that she had talked to Magri by telephone. She meant that she had talked to Magri in Mendoza that morning, but the Magri family interpreted it to mean she had talked to him that evening and that the plane was safe.

At about 10:00 p.m., this word reached the television and radio stations. Along the way, it had been expanded and distorted. When the bulletins went out over the air, they said the Fairchild had been found. It had landed in Curico—or some town south of Santiago. When all the families heard this news, they wept with joy.

Cibilis Juan, father of the club president

Daniel Juan, telephoned Maquirriain to talk about the good news. He invited Maquirriain to his home for a drink to celebrate. When Maquirriain arrived, he found Bobby's father, Valdimir Jaugust, and Daniel Juan. They happily toasted the end of four hours of great tension.

* * *

Gustavo Nicolich's father, the architect, was going through the same ups and downs, hopes raised, hopes dashed, hopes raised again. He received first word at his office, then hurried home, where (like many parents) he tried without success to get some official word from the Air Force. Like the others, he believed at first that the plane was on the way back from Santiago, but Roy Harley, Sr., called and told him that the plane had stopped in Mendoza and had disappeared with all the boys en route to Santiago. When the news about the plane being found safe in Curico came on the radio, Nicolich called a brother-in-law who worked on a newspaper. The brother-in-law could not confirm this news. Half an hour later, he phoned back to say that the plane definitely had *not* been found in Curico. The Curico story was all wrong.

At about 11:00 that night, the radio and television stations finally got the story straight. The Fairchild had stopped Thurs-

day night in Mendoza. It had taken off for
Santiago at 2:18. It arrived over Curico at
3:24. It disappeared about ten minutes later.
In an initial search, SAR had not found it.

This—the final shock—reverberated
through a hundred or more of the finest,
most affluent households in Uruguay, including that of the President, Juan Bordaberry.
People wept, cried out, prayed or became
comatose. The families divided about evenly:
half had hope the boys would be found, half
gave up hope in the first hours. Seler Parrado
was among the latter; he was certain that he
had lost his wife, his daughter and his son.

Among those who had hope, none was
more optimistic than the painter Páez Vilaró.
Immediately after confirming the news that
the plane and his son were lost, he set off
for Santiago to help in the search, never
doubting for an instant that he would find
his son alive and well. Other fathers, brothers, uncles, friends—those who had hope or
felt a duty—followed him in a steady stream.

CHAPTER TEN

A Classic Reversal of Literature

On Friday night, after the first air search missions turned in negative results, Major Ivanovic, commanding SAR, mobilized for an all-out search. SAR would do that for any lost aircraft. But Ivanovic, like all Chileans, felt a special kinship for the Uruguayans. Besides that, it was an Air Force plane, full of the sons of Uruguay's finest families, including relatives of the President. No effort would be spared; no stone left unturned.

To assist in operations and planning, Ivanovic called on two Chilean Air Force cohorts, both former commanders of SAR. These were Majors Carlos Garcia and Jorge Massa. Garcia and Massa were without question the finest, bravest and most skilled pilots in the Chilean Air Force. Both flew helicopters and fixed-wing aircraft. Massa had been official pilot for two previous presidents of Chile and was currently official pilot for Dr. Salvador Allende.

By the time Garcia and Massa arrived, Ivanovic had obtained the official tapes from Mendoza and Santiago Controls. The three pilots sat down to analyze the tapes, jotting notes, consulting aerial charts. They saw at once that if the Fairchild had reported Malargue correctly—had not taken a shortcut and faked the report—there was no way he could have reached Curico as reported. They did not believe that the pilots, both military, would have faked the reports and taken a shortcut.

The three pilots then plotted the true track of the Fairchild, figuring in the headwinds. They calculated, correctly, that the plane had turned north at Planchon or just beyond. It had flown at least six minutes, perhaps seven. On a map, they drew a square, twenty miles on a side. At the top center of the square was Mount Paloma, 15,912 feet. At bottom center was Mount Tinguiririca, 15,400 feet. On the bottom right was Mount Sosneado, 16,929 feet. On the top right was Mount Overo, 15,638 feet. The whole left side of the square was occupied by the mass of unexplored glacial ice lying between Paloma and Tinguiririca. In sum: one of the most inaccessible, roughest sections of the Andes, covered in most places by twenty feet of snow, deposited there by the storms that had made for the worst winter in forty years.

"Here," Jorge Massa said, pointing to the square with a pencil, "is where we concentrate the search."

Unknown to them, the fuselage of the Fairchild lay within the square, near the bottom line, between Tinguiririca on the west

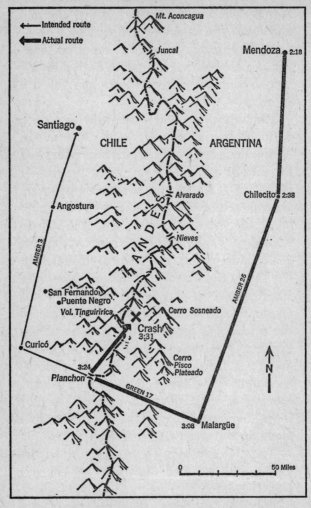

The flight's intended route, the actual route
and the crash site.

and Sosneado on the east. Exact position: 34 degrees 47 minutes south; 70 degrees 13 minutes west.

Having determined the area in which to concentrate the search, SAR then alerted another rescue organization, the *Cuerpo de Socorro Andino de Chile*—the Andes Rescue Group of Chile—CSA.

CSA is one of the most remarkable rescue units in the world. Its members, all volunteers, are skilled mountain climbers with years of experience in the Andes. The group maintains a headquarters in downtown Santiago where there is a member on telephone duty 24-hours a day, and a duty patrol sleeping in a dormitory. The CSA members are specialists in rescuing people lost in the mountains: sightseers, serious climbers (who must register with CSA before climbing), victims of aircraft crashes.

The CSA had long worked hand-in-glove with SAR. Its members had participated in countless aircraft hunts, earthquake disasters and other emergencies. It was a group of CSA men who reached the burned wreckage of the aircraft that crashed with the Green Cross soccer team in April, 1961. They removed the 29 burned bodies.

The CSA responded, as always, willingly and unselfishly. The duty patrol—businessmen, teachers, doctors, lawyers—checked in with SAR. They would fly in the search planes, skilled eyes watching for any unusual sign in the snow or the rocks. Many had years of experience in such searches, and no one was better qualified or knew the terrain better. They were willing to assume all the risks the SAR pilots assumed, without pay, merely in the hope that they might make a contribution.

The next morning, Saturday, October 14, three Chilean Air Force planes temporarily on loan to SAR took off at 10:35. Each had on board a member of CSA. The three planes flew for two hours and five minutes, each searching a different grid in the 20-mile square. An hour later, two more planes were airborne. The five Chilean planes were joined by three Argentine F-86 jets that took off from Mendoza and searched the Andes on the Argentine side. Between noon and one o'clock, three more planes, including a private aircraft and a police aircraft, took to the air.

While these planes were airborne, the artist Páez Vilaró, a friend from São Paulo—Melo Machado, Gustavo Nicolich, and several Uruguayan journalists, including the brilliant Omar Piva of Montevideo's *El Diario*, arrived at SAR headquarters. Major Ivanovic at first was startled, then impressed by Páez Vilaró, a handsome man of 44 years, who was at once immensely charming, brilliant, persuasive and emotional. Páez told Ivanovic that he felt a deep intuition—a religious faith—

that his son was alive and that he would find him. He insisted that he and Nicolich, who likewise held hope, be permitted to join the search flights on SAR aircraft.

This was a situation unique in Ivanovic's experience. Ordinarily, parents and relatives were content to let SAR do the searching; few were willing to risk their necks in flights over the Andes. Now Ivanovic was confronted by not only two Uruguayan fathers but three Uruguayan reporters as well. Ivanovic, a cautious military man, was overwhelmed by Páez Vilaró. He gave his consent. The President's pilot, Jorge Massa, would fly the aircraft, a DC-6.

Later, Omar Piva recalled: "I have known Páez Vilaró for years. He is flamboyant, like Salvador Dali. Often I wondered if he wasn't simply a publicity hound, a hustler trying to drive up the value of his paintings. I wondered, briefly, if his appearance in Santiago that day might not be another publicity stunt, an appalling lapse of taste. I say briefly because I was immediately confronted with another Páez Vilaró: he was completely real, completely genuine, absolutely convinced that his son was alive. It was a mystical thing, as though he had established some psychic communication with the boys on the mountain. He could not be persuaded to take a realistic view, admit to the possibility that his son might be dead. It was a classic rever-

sal of literature: the father hunting for the
son rather than the son hunting for the father. I—and everybody else on the plane—
was profoundly moved."

The big DC-6—stripped of seats for cargo
carrying—took off in the late afternoon, a
bad time for flying the Andes. Páez and
Nicolich, Omar Piva and the other reporters
took station at windows. The pilot, Massa,
flew down to Planchon, checking communications with Santiago Control, then turned
north and flew back and forth over the
square, concentrating on the volcano Tinguiririca. The men at the windows stared
down at the bright snow and ice and were
temporarily afflicted by snow blindness.
Massa kept the plane at 16,000 feet to avoid
the late afternoon wind currents boiling
down through the canyons. Even so, it was
turbulent.

From that altitude, there was no way to
get a good look into the canyons and gorges.
The hope was that they might see a signal
created by the boys: smoke, the glint of a
mirror, or perhaps a cross—the universal dis-
tress signal—stamped out in the snow. With
luck, the sun might reflect off an aluminum
wing.

They saw nothing.

In all, on that Saturday, SAR mounted fifteen missions, utilizing twelve aircraft. They
flew a total of 36 hours and 1 minute, most of

the time within the square. None of the searchers found a trace of the plane. Many returned with the feeling that the search was a hopeless enterprise. It was cold up there—freezing cold. The snow was deeper than anyone had ever seen it. Even if they survived the impact of the crash, how could a group of young boys from Uruguay, none with experience in snow, mountains and high altitudes, be expected to survive in that place without any equipment, warm clothing or food?

CHAPTER ELEVEN

Nine Dead, Eight Missing

On the morning of Saturday, October 14, after the sun rose, a thin light fell into the fuselage of the Fairchild through the port side windows. The Old Christians and supporters, huddled together in the forward fuselage, dead and alive, began to stir and untangle. The injured who were roughed up in the untangling moaned and cried out. Others prayed aloud, thanking God for salvation.

Some of the boys went outside the plane where the dead had been laid out. They inspected the awesome landscape. To the west, east and south, they saw huge mountains, covered with deep snow. The Fairchild had come to rest in a funnel-shaped area, surrounded on three sides by lower peaks, including the one the plane had hit. It was a grim, gray day, freezing cold, deathly silent. Patches of fog lay in the low areas and the overcast skies seemed to hold promise of more snow.

Those who lived now began to think more clearly and to follow human instincts. The first task was to bury the dead—to remove from sight as quickly as possible the horribly mangled, blood-soaked bodies that had once been happy, carefree friends. All who were able participated in this gruesome chore. The surviving medical students, Canessa, Storm and Zerbino, had, of course, seen or worked on cadavers at school. However, many of the boys had never seen a dead body before.

The boys dragged the dead to a level place near the plane and buried them in the snow. They had a difficult time removing the body of co-pilot Lagurara from the cockpit. They were unable to take out the body of the plane commander, Ferradas, because it was tightly jammed in the right seat by the instrument panel and wheel. They left the body where it was.

In all, there were nine dead in the fuselage — three of them women. They were:

1. The pilot, Ferradas
2. The co-pilot, Lagurara
3. Dr. Nicola
4. Esther Nicola
5. Graziela Mariani
6. Eugenia Parrado, Fernando's mother
7. Fernando Vazquez
8. Felipe Maquirriain
9. Julio Martinez-Lamas

There were eight "missing." One of these was Carlos Valeta, who was seen the day before running down the hillside, then disappearing into the snow. The other seven were:

1. Ramon Martinez, navigator
2. Ovidio Ramirez, steward
3. Guido Magri
4. Gaston Costemalle
5. Daniel Shaw
6. Alejo Hounié
7. Juan Carlos Menendez

The boys supposed that all these people, like Valeta, had been sitting in the tail, with or without seatbelts fastened, and had fallen with the tail at the top of the mountain where the plane hit the rock. They supposed that some of them had survived the crash and were huddled in the tail section, as they had huddled in the fuselage.

In fact, all the missing were dead. Counting these eight, a total of seventeen people died in the crash or during the hours that followed. There were 28 survivors—all at the fuselage.

The boys buried eight of the nine bodies at the fuselage, leaving Ferradas in the cockpit. The graves were shallow indentations in the snow, scooped out with luggage and scraps of metal from the plane. After the bodies had been stripped of clothing (which was added to the supply for the survivors) they were placed in the graves, then covered with snow. It was exhausting but necessary work. Most of the boys were Catholic; they believed firmly in a decent Christian burial.

During the macabre funeral, one of the boys noticed that the body of Fernando Parrado, believed to be dead, was not so cold as the others. Nor had rigor mortis set in. They called for Canessa. Canessa—disbelieving his own senses—felt a pulse. Parrado was alive! He had survived the night in the snow in a thin sport shirt. They dragged Parrado back into the fuselage. They dressed him in warm clothing. Some of the boys massaged him to revive circulation. Parrado remained unconscious, but alive. It was, the boys believed, a miracle. God had not wanted Parrado dead.

After the funeral, Canessa and the other medical students turned to help the eight or ten badly injured. Canessa looked for a first-aid kit. There was none. If there had been one, it must have been in the tail section. Canessa improvised, bathing wounds with after-shave lotion and cologne found in the luggage.

One case that worried Canessa was "The Brute," Platero, who had been impaled by the aluminum rod. It seemed necessary to Canessa to "operate" on Platero, to sew up the wound so that Platero's intestines would not push out again. He found a needle and thread in the luggage—a woman's sewing kit. He bathed the wound with cologne, then sewed it with the thread.

Among the most seriously injured were Francisco Abal and Susana Parrado. Abal had broken bones and internal injuries. Susana, badly smashed up, had many broken bones in her legs and was in deep shock, babbling incoherently and incessantly. Canessa, helped by Storm and Zerbino, did all he could to make them comfortable, filling air sickness bags with snow to use as ice bags.

Three boys had mangled legs: Echavarren, with his right calf ripped open, Alvaro Mangino and Alfredo Delgado with broken bones. The medical students could do little to help Echavarren (who bravely declined help anyway and insisted on changing his own bandages), but they put splints on Mangino and Delgado.

For those with contusions and head wounds, little could be done. In this category fell the mechanic, Roque, and the economics students José Pedro Algorta, who had visited Mendoza University with Felipe Maquirriain, now dead, and Arturo Nogueira. Algorta remembered nothing of the first five days on the mountain. For quite a long time, Nogueira behaved abnormally, as though he were "a little nuts."

After the dead had been buried and the

injured attended to, the boys now turned to the problem of their own survival: shelter and food.

First, shelter.

The fuselage of the Fairchild was still a shambles of broken seats, canted over at 45 degrees. There were holes in the skin, some windows missing and, of course, the gaping snow-filled hole in the rear, facing uphill. First, the boys took the seats out to make more room. Then they removed interior paneling and laid it out to make a flat, rather than a round floor. (The false floor also lifted them from the dirty bilge water of melting snow.) They laid out the foam rubber of the seats for mattresses. They closed off the rear end by stacking the luggage then packing snow behind it. They taped the windows in place with electrical tape and plugged the holes in the fuselage with old, useless clothing. They made a tunnel in the snow to go in and out of the fuselage, and an inner door to close off the tunnel at night. When they were finished, the fuselage was so air-tight, they had to install a "snorkel" or air scoop, improvised from a piece of plastic pipe from the cabin heating ducts.

Second, food. Thanks to the overnight stop in Mendoza, which had generated many idle hours and therefore much shopping, the boys had a small—very small—storehouse of goodies: chocolate bars, tins of fish and fish paste, cheese, marmalade, some sweets, and, in total, about forty quarts of wine. The mechanical engineering student Roy Harley, who was unhurt, was delegated to "ration" the food.

Surrounded by billions of tons of snow, the survivors had no shortage of water. At first, they scooped it up and sucked it. But then someone remembered he had heard that sucking snow was not good: it could lead to stomach cramps or perhaps to pneumonia. Clearly, it would be better to melt the snow. They had fire—matches and cigarette lighters —but very little paper or anything else to burn.

One boy, rummaging through a suitcase, found an enormous sum of money: two million pesos (roughly $2,000), perhaps the money Graziela was taking to her daughter for a wedding present. Since the money belonged to no one alive, and could do them little good where they were, the boys built a fire with it to melt snow. "It must be the most expensive glass of water in history," José Luis Inciarte joked.

After the immediate needs of survival had been attended to, the boys then turned their minds toward a single thought: rescue. They believed it would come very soon. They consulted the maps found in the cockpit. They found the city of Curico and traced a line north toward Santiago. They figured they must have crashed in the mountains east of the town of San Fernando, up from the village of Punte Negro, where the tan coloring on the map showed 7,000 feet, the altitude the altimeter indicated. Not more than ten miles to green grass—and civilization. Surely the co-pilot had radioed his position over Curico. There would be a radio log. The rescue planes could figure their exact position and search it. After they had been found from the air, the rescuers could send in helicopters or perhaps ground teams. The boys believed it would only be a matter of one, two or three days before they were saved from this white hell.

Always, the orientation of rescue and escape was westward—toward Chile—based on the incorrect information supplied by Lagurara before he died and on the false altimeter reading. No one ever considered looking east toward Argentina, or that the wreck could possibly have occurred in Argentina. But it had. And, ironically, they had crashed less than five miles (as the crow flies) from a summer resort hotel, Termas. It was located downhill and to the west, a day and a half or two days hike in the snow. It was closed, but there was firewood, canned food and maps.

It was unfortunate in one sense that Lagurara lived. Had he been killed instantly in the crash, unable to pass along his incorrect information, the boys might have done more calculating on their own. They knew the time of take-off and the time of the crash. Using the maps and the Fairchild handbooks in the cockpit, they could have plotted their approximate course from Mendoza to Malargue to Planchon and the fatal turn north. They might possibly have arrived at a more accurate position of the crash on their own and oriented themselves toward the east— Argentina—the correct solution. In two days they might have located the hotel.

However, that was never to be. Lagurara's incorrect deathbed utterances would lead to more deaths, more unspeakable horror.

CHAPTER TWELVE

SAR: *Optimism in Public, Pessimism in Private*

In SAR headquarters at Los Cerrillos airport outside Santiago, Major Ivanovic, swamped by frantic parents, relatives and friends of the Old Christians, projected optimism and tolerated the Monday-morning quarterbacks with consummate diplomacy. But behind the scenes, in conference with Majors Garcia and Massa, who were helping mastermind the search, he was pessimistic. The weather had turned foul. There was more bad weather on the way; it would probably bring more snow in the Andes. Forty-one and half hours of search on Friday and Saturday had turned up nothing.

Then came encouraging news. On Sunday, October 15, a miner, working in a mine near Planchon, reported seeing the Fairchild pass over the mine, then turn north. Since this was the first confirmation of the flight plan—until then only a theory—Major Ivanovic sent a helicopter to pick up the miner. His name was Camilo del Carmen Figueroa, and he was an illiterate mountain man.

Major Garcia asked Figueroa for details. The miner said he saw the plane "falling with engines in flames." He described it as a

111

four-engine plane painted red. Garcia had
real doubts about the miner's story, but SAR
mobilized police near the mine to go from
house to house and make inquiries. This was
no small undertaking. The snow in Planchon
was deep; the trails in some places were
blocked.

Meanwhile, Ivanovic sent up search planes.
Almost all concentrated near Tinguiririca,
only a few miles from the crash site. One of
the planes reported seeing a column of smoke
and the sun glinting on something. A volun-
teer air-club pilot, Fernando Madrones, a
cousin of Magri's girlfriend, piloting a twin-
engine Cessna owned by Andres Muzard,
went to investigate. On close inspection, it
was found to be smoke boiling up from the
chimney of a coal mine; the sun glints were
caused by the piles of coal.

Madrones, flying low in severe late-after-
noon turbulence, passed directly over the
fuselage of the Fairchild. The boys saw him.
It appeared to them that Madrones dipped
his wings, a signal that they had been seen
and that help was on the way. At the fuselage, there was wild exultation as the boys
waved at the plane, then somber prayer to
thank God for a speedy delivery from that
place.

But Madrones had seen nothing. The boys
were not aware that they were extremely
hard to see from the air. The plane was

white, three-quarters buried in white snow. From several thousand feet up, where Madrones was flying, the boys themselves could not be distinguished, even though some wore dark clothing. Had they known, the boys might have had a fire ready to light in the event a plane came over. Burning some spare clothing or the nosewheel of the plane (then buried in snow) would have sent dense, black smoke aloft. Madrones might have seen it.

In all, Ivanovic mounted nine missions on Sunday. The planes flew a total of 29 hours, 25 minutes. Ivanovic varied the type and search patterns of the aircraft. Some flew high, some low, sweeping down into canyons and gorges. Almost all encountered severe turbulence. The pilots—and the CSA men on the planes—literally risked their own lives to uphold the SAR motto: *Para que otros puedan vivir* ("So that others may live").

On Monday, October 16, Major Ivanovic, with an eye on the bad weather moving up from the southwest, mounted a massive search. Seventeen planes took to the air, including more Argentine jets. They flew 23 missions for a total of 55 hours. The planes concentrated in the area near Mount Paloma and Tinguiririca. Some were equipped with sophisticated aerial photographic equipment. Later the exposed film was developed, enlarged and scrutinized by SAR and CSA experts. Results: negative.

That same day the Uruguayan Air Force
sent the sistership of the lost Fairchild to
Chile. The senior officer on board was Colonel Wilder Jackson. Also on board: Colonel
Luis Charquero, chief of Uruguayan Air
Force flight safety; Captain Enrique Crossa,
Operations Officer of Transport Group 4, to
which the Fairchild had been assigned; and
others. Crossa was a close friend of Ferradas
and Lagurara; he had flown many hours in
the lost plane.

Colonel Jackson's goal was to duplicate the
flight path of the Fairchild, based on all the
information that had been assembled. The
Uruguayans flew the projected route, utilizing both ADF and VOR. They encountered
no abnormalities with the gear. They saw
nothing in the Andes. They landed at Los
Cerrillos on schedule, prepared to join the
SAR search.

On Tuesday, October 17, the bad weather
set in. High winds blew in from the southwest. The search area was soon a mass of
cumulus clouds. The clouds brought electrical
storms and snowfall and extreme turbulence.
The Uruguayan Fairchild remained on the
ground. SAR was able to mount only two
missions that day, flying 2 hours and 45 minutes. Results: negative. Ivanovic spent most
of the day analyzing the aerial photographs
through magnifying machines. Results: negative.

Over the next three days, the weather remained marginal. On Wednesday, October 18, SAR mounted only two missions for a total of three hours searching. On Thursday, he sent out four missions for a little over five hours, including a two-hour mission by the Uruguayan Fairchild, which encountered dangerous turbulence. On Friday, October 20, SAR mounted two missions for about six hours, including another by the Fairchild of two hours and 48 minutes. Each of the search aircraft encountered severe turbulence and heavy snowstorms.

All this time, Chilean police patrols were fanning out from the tiny villages in the foothills, spreading word of the crash to the cowboys and mountain men, making inquiries. SAR received no precise information of the number of days expended in this effort, but Major Ivanovic reported the total was "substantial." Except for the miner in Planchon, no one had seen anything. The miner's story was ultimately discounted because the technical details (such as color of the aircraft and number of engines) did not square with known facts.

On Saturday, October 21, Major Ivanovic announced to the Uruguayan chargé d'affaires, Cesar Charlone, to Colonel Wilder Jackson, the parents and newsmen, that SAR was terminating the search. It had gone on for eight days. In all, SAR had called on 55 aircraft (44 from Chile, six from Argentina, the others private, police and commercial) which flew a total of 61 missions for 142 hours and 30 minutes. None had found a trace of the plane or the survivors—if any.

Ivanovic did not say so in public, but privately he believed the Fairchild was lost with all hands. The odds of anybody being alive were a million to one. The plane had crashed in the worst section of the Andes, probably in an area where no man had ever been or was likely to go, even in the finest summer weather. It had been snowing hard for days. The snow would have covered the wreckage and any signals that might have been made. How could anybody live in those freezing temperatures without heat or special cold-weather gear? What would they *eat*? As Ivanovic knew, the Fairchild carried no food.

Most of the parents and friends of the boys who had been in Santiago second-guessing the SAR search agreed with Major Ivanovic. Considering the weather, the search had been thorough. SAR had done all that could be reasonably done. They issued a public statement of gratitude and returned, by ones and twos, to Montevideo.

Gilberto Regules had remained in Santiago for many days, observing the SAR operations. When he returned to Montevideo, he was pessimistic, reflecting the SAR view. He confided his views to his father, stating that he intended to call on each of the families and break the bad news. His father advised against this. It was a despairing thing to do. Better, he said, to tell a little white lie. Don't kill hope where there was hope. Let it die of itself, in the way that was best for each family.

Regules went from family to family, telling all that he had seen and heard in Santiago, giving his story an optimistic shading. He found many families—perhaps half—believed their sons were still alive and that they would ultimately be found. After a time, Regules began to believe his own story. It might be true after all. His friends might be alive. His father, believing that his son was driving himself crazy with all this talk, ordered him to the ranch so he might forget.

There was a reason for the hope Regules found in some homes. Some of the Uruguayan mothers had made contact with a famous Dutch seer named Gerard Croiset, who had been an advisor to Queen Juliana of the Netherlands. At their request, Croiset went into a trance, emerged and reported to the Uruguayans (in a series of expensive overseas telephone calls) that he could "see" the plane, crashed in the Andes, near a lake, wings and engines sheared off, fuselage intact. He could also "see" people alive inside the fuselage.

Many parents, including Daniel Shaw and

117

Seler Parrado, considered the Croiset visions nonsense. But Uruguayan women—like most Latin women—have a heavy streak of spiritualism and mysticism. They believe in miracles, psychic powers, seers. Besides, they had one irrefutable argument in their favor: hadn't a famous Chilean seer precisely located the lost plane of the Green Cross soccer team?

Not even the tough-minded professionals of the CSA could deny that. They were realists, not spiritualists, but it was an undeniable fact that the Chilean seer had found that plane.

So the search for the boys, now conducted solely by some of the parents, went on.

CHAPTER THIRTEEN

Ingenuity, Religion, Despair

Deep in the Andes, the 28 survivors who believed they had been spotted on Sunday, October 15, awaited rescue on Monday. When the sun came up, those who were able crawled outside the plane. The sun reflected off the brilliant white snow, temporarily blinding some. As it rose higher, the heat was as intense and unbearable as the cold of the night. The boys stripped off their shirts and soaked up the sun. By 11:30 a.m., it was no longer possible to remain outside the plane. They crawled back inside until 3:00 p.m., when the sun began to go down behind the peaks in the west. By 6:00 or 6:30, the cold had set in again and they had to return to the fuselage. Thus the elements set the daily routine.

As they awaited rescue, the survivors damned the Uruguayan Air Force on many points. Why was the fuselage of a plane that regularly flew the Andes painted white to blend with snow? Why not brilliant orange or crimson? Why was there no medicine chest in the forward end of the plane? Or at least a first-aid kit? Where was the emergency gear? The flares, the smoke bombs, the very

Survive!

pistols? A parachute to spread in the snow? Why wasn't the plane equipped with an automatic device that would send out an emergency signal on which rescue planes and ground parties could "home"?

The only piece of emergency gear the boys found was a heavy stainless-steel ax, fitted in a sleeve behind the pilot's seat in the cockpit. It was there to enable the crew to hack through the fuselage in case the doors were jammed in a crash.

Inside the fuselage, there was at least one reason to cheer. Fernando Parrado, who had been left outside the first night with the dead, regained consciousness after three days. He was weak, but alive. His mother was dead. His sister, Susana, badly injured, still babbled incoherently and seemed to be losing ground steadily. The hope was that the rescue would save at least two of the three Parrados and Francisco Abal, who was also in serious condition.

The other injured seemed to be improving. They were Alvaro Mangino (broken leg), Alfredo Delgado (broken leg), Rafael Echavarren (mangled calf), Enrique Platero (abdomen wound from the aluminum rod) and Antonio Vizintín (cuts on arm). The mechanic, Roque, and José Algorta were still in deep shock.

The other eighteen survivors, which included team supporter Javier Methol, 36, and

120

his wife Liliana, divided into teams to carry out the essentials for survival. Roy Harley distributed the rations of food. The medical students—Roberto Canessa, Gustavo Zerbino and Diego Storm—attended the injured. Carlos Páez distributed aspirin and Alka Seltzer found in the luggage to the injured.

Adolfo Strauch and his cousin, Eduardo Strauch, helped with the "housing," divising ways to make the fuselage more livable. In addition, Adolfo, nicknamed "the Inventor," devised a means of utilizing the intense heat of the sun to melt snow for drinking water. It was packed in the bright aluminum seat backings, then drained off into empty wine bottles and little jars. Inasmuch as the goal was two liters per person per day, snow melting became an enormous (and boring) chore in which many participated. Adolfo also devised sun glasses (made of pieces of tinted plastic found in the plane) to prevent further cases of snow blindness.

Others helped manufacture cold weather clothing from the seat covers, which were cut away along the seams. The pieces of seat covers were then pieced together with wire found in the plane. The boys made "blankets" resembling ponchos, with a hole in the center, hoods with drawstrings made of wire and mittens.

The eighteen uninjured included many Old Christians, like Roberto Canessa, who had been in excellent physical shape when they crashed. Canessa and others, believing it essential to stay in good physical condition, engaged in daily isometric exercises. They recalled the case of the British diplomat, Geoffrey Jackson, who was captured by Uruguayan Tupomoros and kept locked in tight quarters for many months. He survived, the story went, by keeping himself physically fit.

Sleeping—passing the night—was still the greatest trial of all. There were only about fifteen feet of usable fuselage. In order to keep from freezing, the twenty-eight survivors, including both injured and fit, had to sleep in "stacked" formation: legs intertwined, or draped over someone else's body. Often, a leg would get cold and bring on a cramp. To get rid of the cramp, the boy had to stretch his leg. When he stretched his leg, he usually kicked someone in the face. This brought on a cry of pain from the boy kicked, and sometimes curses and blows, a wild melee into which several others would be dragged. As a result of these fights, so much anger and hostility built up during the nights that they instituted a rule that everybody had to shake hands all around every morning.

*　*　*

The bad weather set in on Tuesday. Snow fell, terrifying electrical storms boiled through the area. The boys watched the skies for air-

craft, but none were flying. They believed
the rescuers were waiting out the bad
weather, or that they were sending in an expedition by land. During the snowstorms,
which set off small avalanches, the survivors
huddled inside the fuselage; only the water
detail went outside. Prayer became ritualized: every morning and evening the boys
said a community rosary, using a rosary with
wooden beads that had been given to Carlos
Páez by his mother. With 25 hungry teen-
agers to feed (three of the injured were unable to eat), the small food and wine supply
dwindled rapidly. Some of the boys became
weak and lightheaded. All drank water to kill
the hunger pangs.

During one night, Francisco Abal, one of
the team's best players, died lying atop Susana Parrado, trying to keep *her* warm. This
new death caused a wave of profound sad-
ness, especially for his uncle and aunt, the
elder Methols. On the day following, his
body was removed from the plane and buried with the eight others. Javier Methol conducted the service.

When the rescuers failed to appear, the
boys began to think about the tail section
that had been chopped off at the top of the
mountain. They did not know it sailed on
down the mountainside below them; they
were sure it was still at the top. It contained
the plane's galley and much luggage. There

would be food in the galley and maybe food in the luggage, more chocolates and sweets bought in Mendoza. There might even be survivors. They decided to send an expedition to find the tail and whatever could be found.

The mechanic, Roque, added another incentive. The tail, he said, contained the two big nickel-cadmium batteries. If these could be brought down the hill on a sled (they were very heavy), it might be possible to connect them to the plane's radio transmitter which had survived intact but had no electrical power. If so, they could send out a call for help.

Roque added a second incentive. There was a medical chest in the tail. It contained antibiotics, amphetamines, tranquillizers, bandages, tape, etc. This was news of prime importance to Roberto Canessa. Susana Parrado, he feared, had gangrene in both legs. If it wasn't too late, the antibiotics might help her. They would also help the other injured ones.

For all these reasons, finding the tail now became imperative. But how could they climb to the top of the mountain in that deep snow? Hadn't three of the boys seen Carlos Valeta fall into a soft spot and disappear? Since that time, more snow had fallen. There must be many more soft spots. There was also the ever-present danger of avalanche.

The ingenuity of Adolfo Strauch, "the Inventor," rose to the occasion. He designed two vital pieces of equipment: snowshoes and safety lines. He made the snowshoes from the foam rubber seat cushions. He made the safety lines from the seatbelts and the nylon webbing that formed the luggage compartment in the forward end of the cabin. In tests carried out near the fuselage, the shoes worked. Nobody sank in the snow.

The group picked four boys to make this first major expedition, those who were considered the most fit physically. They were the law student Numa Turcatti; Carlos Páez; "the Inventor," Adolfo Strauch; and Roberto Canessa.

On the morning of Friday, October 20, the last day of the SAR search, the four boys, linked together by the safety lines, wearing snowshoes and carrying aluminum poles for balance, set off for the top of the mountain. One of them carried the heavy stainless-steel emergency ax. The weather was foul: the sky was overcast, strong winds blew through the funnel-shaped area. The four boys, bent against the wind, started uphill walking carefully, shouting encouragement. Those left behind, such as Gustavo Nicolich, marveled at their courage.

They did not go far. The weather worsened, the air was thin, each step forward required enormous effort. The wind blew hard and the four boys were soon freezing cold. After a few hours, they gave up and returned to the plane. This pioneering effort demonstrated one essential fact: launching an expedition of some distance in that environment was a large and dangerous enterprise, not to be embarked upon lightly. They would need warmer clothing, perhaps sleeping bags in case they were waylaid by a storm and couldn't return to the fuselage.

The following morning, October 21, the day SAR officially called off the search, Susana Parrado, who had developed gangrene in both legs, was obviously dying. Carlos Páez gave her a rubdown, but it did not help. She died in her brother's arms that day. They carried her body out and buried it in the snow beside her mother. Susana brought the total number of bodies in this bizarre cemetery to ten.

Fernando Parrado was distraught and confused. In his grief, he could not comprehend why God had spared him, and taken away his devoted mother and sister. In time he evolved what he believed to be the answer. He had been spared for a specific purpose: to take charge, to save the rest of the boys from death. He was overcome by messianic zeal, a single-minded determination to save himself and the others and to return to his father.

That evening Gustavo Nicolich sat down

and wrote a joint letter to his parents, his younger sisters and brother, his sister's boyfriend, Juan, and his girlfriend, Rosina:

I am writing this eight days after the plane crashed in the Andes. We are in a wonderful place, closed by mountains with a lake behind which will melt when summer comes. We are all right. At this moment, we are twenty-six. . . . But we are always helping and morale is good. Roy Harley, Diego Storm, Roberto Canessa, Carlos Páez and I are perfectly well but a bit thinner and bearded.

Last Sunday two planes flew over us —twice each—so we are quite convinced that we are going to be rescued. The only thing that raises doubt is that the planes didn't reverse course, and maybe they didn't see us. Our faith in God is incredible. I know people in the same situation as ours felt the same, but our faith is stronger. Perhaps in Montevideo, you are asking how we are living? The truth is the plane isn't in perfect shape. It isn't a big hotel but it will be very soon.

We have plenty of water because we make it constantly. Food, well I was lucky because I have a tin of canned fish, three tins of fish paste, some chocolate and two little bottles of whiskey.

Of course there isn't a lot of food but we can survive.

During the day, when the weather is good, we can stay out of the plane until 6 p.m. (now it is cloudy). Usually we stay in the hotel (plane) and only those looking for snow go out. The rooms are not too comfortable. There is only one room for 26 people, but at least it's something.

The only part of the plane remaining is the cabin because the wings fell off. To make room, we took all the seats out and took the covers off to make blankets. As you can see, we are improving our comfort.

I miss you very much and constantly ask God that if He wants to take me to Him, at least let me see you once more. I can't forget (Rosina) how I arrived every night at your house and I saw your mother knitting or mending something. Nor can I forget you, father, when you took me to college or when we talked on Saturdays (because, the truth is, I saw you seldom on the other days and I was to blame, of course).

Rosina, you can't imagine how much I miss you. Words can't tell, but luckily I have your picture in my wallet and every night before going to bed I kiss it as if I were in your house saying good-night. The only thing I want right now is to get married, if you want to. But I can't stand to think about that because it makes me cry and I was told not to cry because I will lose water (it's incredible, no?).

To my younger sisters and brother, Monica, Raquel and Ale, you also can imagine how I miss you. You are the only thing I have. I am going to try to survive if God helps me in order to see you again.

Juan [Monica's boyfriend], you try to be the oldest brother I couldn't ever be and please look after Monica, my parents and my Rosina.

We are always making jokes about food. Everyday somebody orders his meals as though in a restaurant . . . I miss a lot of Rosina's family and friends but if I had to choose, I would choose the meals prepared by Blanca [Rosina's cook] and the glasses of milk at my house. Now I believe Montevideo and my house are the best places and I want to see them again. To be with you, Rosina, every night.

Near me are Daniel Maspons, Diego Storm, Arturo Nogueira and Alvaro Mangino. We were just saying it was very strange that the rescuers hadn't appeared yet. But I think we are in a very inac-

cessible place and that we can only be
seen by land. The weather has not ben
very god and we had some little avalanches. The rescuers must be waiting a
little more. This thought and our faith
in God keeps us at ease. We pray every
night and every morning. One of us
begins the prayers with his own words.
This is a way of sharing our faith. Each
night, we all tell our funniest stories—
about fathers- and mothers-in-law that I
will tell you someday. I hope it will be
very soon.

The most incredible thing is a friend
I have met here—"Moncho" Sabella. We
sleep together and hold hands as the
weather is so cold we constantly breathe
on each other to give heat on the coldest
nights. If it hadn't been for him I would
have died the first night. The plane was
broken and the weather was very cold.
That was the night in which the bigger
group of people died. . . .

Well, I have to leave you because it's
nearly evening and there is a lot of work
to do. A great big kiss to all of you and I
will see you if God is willing. If it is
not to be, the only thing I ask is for you
to be brave and don't worry about me.
I'm sure God will take me with Him. To
you, Rosina, I don't know how to tell

you I love you, that I adore you, and
that I miss you terribly. . . .

Gustavo

While Gustavo was writing his letter, one
of the boys, scrounging near the plane, made
a great find: a transistor radio. It was in perfect condition and the batteries were strong.
erty.

On the following morning, Sunday, October 22, they took it outside the fuselage at
7:00 and tuned it to a news broadcast. The
first news they heard was an official an-
nouncement from SAR: the search for the
Uruguayan Fairchild, lost with 45 people,
had been called off.

This news plunged many into new depths
of depression. Some cried. Gustavo Nicolich
had the opposite reaction. He was relieved.
He said, "Thank God! Now we can stop all
this waiting around and try to get out of here
by ourselves."

CHAPTER FOURTEEN

The Man Who Owned Tinguiririca

Among the parents who carried on the search in Chile was the artist Carlos Páez Vilaró. Those in Montevideo relayed news to him of the visions of the Dutch seer Croiset. The seer's visions reinforced Vilaró's determination to find his son. He set up a headquarters in the Hotel Crillon in downtown Santiago. It was an ideal setting for Vilaró. It put him close to government agencies, libraries, geographical and geological societies which could provide information on the Andes.

In spite of the general strike in Chile, which disrupted everything and brought on rioting in the streets, people began to congregate in the headquarters. Among these were Dr. Luis Surraco, father of Roberto Canessa's fiancée, Miguel Garderes, 20, a close friend of many of the boys, who had been hiking in Peru when he received word of the disaster, and others.

As a first step, Vilaró made it his business to become an expert on the Andes as rapidly as possible. He skimmed through every book on the Andes he could lay his hands on. In one, he came across the name of Joaquin

Gandarillas, mentioned as an expert on the area where SAR believed the plane had crashed. There were about twenty Gandarillas in the Santiago telephone book, but no Joaquin. Vilaró began going down the list, name by name. Eventually, he made contact with Joaquin.

"I am the father of one of the boys lost in the Uruguayan plane near the volcano Tinguiririca," Vilaró told him. "I understand you are an expert on the area. Would you help me, please?"

Few could deny Vilaró. Gandarillas, braving the rioters in the streets and police tear gas, made his way to the Crillon. Vilaró greeted a portly, middle-aged man who spoke in a soft voice, giving facts in a precise manner. He had been a wealthy landowner, a farmer and cattle raiser. The Gandarillas family had owned huge tracts of land in the foothills and in the Andes. The Allende government, in its farm nationalization program, had seized most of the good land in the foothills, but the family still owned vast tracts in the Andes, including most of the mountain Tinguiririca.

"You own the *mountain*?" Vilaró asked in astonishment.

"Most of it," Gandarillas replied. "And the grazing land to the south and west, toward Puente Negro."

Vilaró bombarded Gandarillas with questions. Were there roads into Tinguiririca? What were the conditions? Did people live there? Could the boys survive the cold? Would Gandarillas arrange for them to go there by land? Would he accompany them?

Gandarillas was moved by Vilaró's faith that he could find his son alive. He agreed to do all he could to help form a search expedition by land, but cautioned Vilaró that the snows had been heavy that winter and conditions in the mountain would be dangerous.

On Friday, October 20, the last day of the SAR air search—and the day the four boys attempted to climb to the top of the mountain—the expedition set off in a taxi from the Crillon Hotel. It included Vilaró, Joaquin Gandarillas, Dr. Surraco, the boy Miguel Garderes, plus another young friend of the Old Christians. Vilaró had not slept. He had received five telephone calls from Montevideo during the night from mothers who had been in touch with the Dutch seer. The seer still insisted that he "saw" people alive inside the fuselage.

As the car headed south for San Fernando, the strike which had immobilized Chile was reaching its peak intensity. There was not another car on the highway. The road was littered with barbed nails, thrown there by truck strikers to impede traffic. Once when they stopped for information, strikers charged the taxi, threatening the driver. When he explained the reason for the expedition, the strikers backed off and wished them well.

Along the way, Vilaró's thoughts were fixed on the Dutch seer and his vision. He talked incessantly about him. Gandarillas was attentive but uneasy. He did not believe in such things. He was concerned that the police and other officials they had to contact that day might be put off by talk of visions. Gently, diplomatically, Gandarillas suggested it might be better not to mention the seer. Vilaró agreed.

They stopped first at the San Fernando Aero Club, located in a cow pasture just north of the town, and met the man in charge. Seeing half a dozen aircraft parked in and around the hangar, Vilaró asked at once if someone could fly him over Tinguiririca. The manager replied it was impossible —the flying conditions were terrible. In such small planes, it would be suicidal.

From the San Fernando airport, they drove east on a dirt road into the foothills of the Andes to the small village of Puente Negro. They stopped at the *retenda*, a small police station manned by Chile's famed *carabiñeros*, men like Canada's Royal Mounted Police, specially trained for duty in the mountains. Only one of the *carabiñeros* knew about the crash. He had seen a brief item in a newspaper.

Vilaró told all he knew, including the SAR theory that the plane had crashed near Tinguiririca. The *carabiñeros* gathered around, somewhat mesmerized by this handsome, charming foreigner who displayed such powerful faith that his son was alive. They were willing to help. If they received clearance from "higher authority," they could form an expedition of *carabiñeros* and some *vaquianos* (mountain men) who knew the trails like the palms of their hands, and go to the top of Tinquiririca. But they could do nothing without the clearance.

From Puente Negro, the expedition drove deeper into the Andes along the narrow and dangerous road leading up to the mountain of El Flaco, a few miles south of Tinguiririca. El Flaco, a summer resort, was closed, buried in snow. But the same road led up to the winter home of Efrain Millan, the chief *vaquiano* for the Gandarillas property.

The home was located at the juncture of two rivers: the Tinguiririca and the Claro. When they got there, Millan's wife had bad news. Her husband was not home. He was at an outpost—a collection of mud huts called Los Maitenes, looking after cattle with her brother, an *arrerio* (cattleman) named Sergio Catalan. Gandarillas talked to Millan's two oldest sons, asking if it was possible to mount an expedition on horseback to Tinguiririca.

"It is impossible," one of the sons said. "The snow is much too deep."

Vilaró asked if they might go on to Los Maitenes, to talk with Millan and Catalan. But the boys said that, too, was impossible. A few days before, an avalanche had closed the road a few miles up the way. They could only drive that far. After that, they would have to go on foot, a long journey in deep snow along hazardous trails, that might take two or three days.

They had gone as far as they could go. The best hope, then, seemed to be the *carabiñeros*. If they could get permission from "higher authority," they could form an expedition. Perhaps Millan and Catalan could join it. Before leaving the Millan home, Vilaró told the wife and the older boys all he knew about the crash and asked them to spread the word to Millan and Catalan and everybody else who lived in the Andes. He requested that if they saw anything unusual in the mountains—smoke, a glint of metal— to inform the *carabiñeros*.

As they were preparing to leave, Vilaró suddenly—and impulsively—turned to one of the sons and asked if he might borrow a horse for a while. When it had been saddled, Vilaró mounted and rode off alone toward the east until stopped by the deep snow. He sat for a time, looking toward the peaks, whistling a special call he and his son shared. There was no reply, not even an echo. Vilaró turned the horse and headed back to the house.

About that same moment, his son, Carlos, alive and well, was 30 miles due east, struggling back to the fuselage after the abortive expedition to the top of the mountain.

On the way out of the hills, the party stopped at an inn for a late lunch. The place was deserted, but they found the owner, who turned out to be Uruguayan. He prepared a meal and served it on the terrace, which looked out on the snow-covered peaks. During the lunch, Vilaró fell into low spirits. As if defeated, he lifted his glass toward the Andes and gave a long and emotional toast which concluded: "So long, boys."

But Vilaró was far from defeated. He shook off the despair and got ready to press on. Their next objective was the police station in Chimbarengo, south of San Fernando, where "higher authority" could authorize the *carabiñeros* at Puente Negro to make a horseback expedition to Tinguiririca.

In Chimbarengo, Joaquin Gandarillas and Páez Vilaró called on the police chief. For the first time, Vilaró met a cold reception. The chief explained that all available police were required to help control the strike. Perhaps later, after the strike. Gandarillas and

Vilaró pleaded. As they talked, the chief grew vague, and finally the matter was left in the air. The strike dragged on and on. No expedition was ever mounted from Puente Negro.

Later, Gandarillas said: "It was most unfortunate, that strike. It caused many problems for everybody and solved nothing. I feel that had it not been for the strike, the *carabiñeros* would have made the expedition to Tinguiririca. In all likelihood, that expedition would have found the boys."

In the weeks that followed, the day with Joaquin Gandarillas was repeated time after time with changing sets of characters. Carlos Páez Vilaró seemed to be everywhere at once, calling on old friends, making new ones: Santiago, San Fernando, Curico, Talca.

"I was like a mailman," he said later, "ringing doorbells, alerting people." He rented big planes, small planes, helicopters, whatever he could find to fly over the foothills and peaks. He organized horseback expeditions. He even talked a group of monks from a school near Talca into going into the foothills to offer a mass for the recovery of the boys.

More and more, Vilaró came to believe all that the seer in Holland told them. In a sense, this was unfortunate. The seer pronounced emphatically that the Fairchild had crashed not where SAR believed it to be

139

(and where it actually was) but southwest of Curico, in the mountains east of Talca. This led Vilaró away from Tinguiririca and up more blind alleys, where, of course, he found no trace of the plane.

CHAPTER FIFTEEN

Decision to Live

On the eighth day on the mountain, the boys ate the last of the food. The final ration was one small piece of chocolate and one spoonful of jam. When the food was gone, they ate the toothpaste. When the toothpaste was gone, they hallucinated. José Inciarte, for example, found a distant rock that resembled a pizza when the sun hit it just right. He imagined that it was smothered in tomato sauce. He said nothing about this find to the others. He feared they might rush there and devour it, leaving nothing for him.

They talked incessantly of food. With the help of Javier Methol, who appeared to have total recall, they drew up a list of Montevideo restaurants and their specialties. They had prime filet with Béarnaise sauce at Montevideo's finest restaurant, Aguilar, an Italian pasta at Morini's, followed by baked Alaska; and a chicken dish at the elegant Victoria Plaza Hotel. They had smorgasbord at the Hotel Bristol in Carrasco. They had succulent barbecued ribs at the Hawaii, a favorite hangout. They had grilled pork and black sausages at Sobrilla. And the fabulous pit-roasted capon at El Galliñero in Punta Gorda. The list grew to fifteen pages.

The hunger was driving them mad. Every waking minute was devoted to talk of and search for food. At that altitude, there was nothing: no lichens, no roots, no vegetation of any kind. Nothing but endless, deep snow and volcanic rock. The only sign of life was an occasional condor flying overhead—a vulture of the Andes, waiting for them to die.

They thought constantly of the tail section and the food it must contain. In spite of the difficulties, Numa Turcatti, who had been a member of the first expedition, organized a second. It was composed of himself, Daniel Maspons and Gustavo Zerbino. Wearing the seat-cushion snowshoes and buckled into safety lines, they set off again for the top of the mountain, struggling up the 80-degree slope, falling in the snow, which, in daytime, became soft and mushy from the intense heat of the sun.

The second expedition got higher than the first—progress of a sort. In a kind of desperate frenzy born of hunger, they searched and searched but, of course, found no sign of the tail. This group had to sleep on the mountainside—the first to remain outside the fuselage overnight since the crash. To keep from freezing, they huddled together and spent the night massaging one another. The following day, they staggered back to the plane empty-handed.

The other boys mounted "mini-expeditions," searching the area near the fuselage for luggage that might contain food. During one of these, Carlos Páez found the trash can from the galley. It was empty. Even so, he brought it back to the fuselage. It was pressed into service by the people melting snow into water.

Each of these expeditions was exhausting. In the thin air, the deep snow, walking a few yards was like walking thirty miles on level land in Uruguay. After eight days these boys, who had been in such fine physical condition when they crashed, were debilitated, hollow-eyed. For some, the instinct to live was ebbing away, replaced by apathy and indifference.

The medical student Roberto Canessa was first to broach the appalling, yet logical, alternative to starvation. He talked about it coolly and scientifically, not pressing but explaining that they were all dying slowly of malnutrition—lack of protein. There was little hope of finding the tail section. Even if they managed to, how long would the food there—if any—last? Certainly not until late spring when the snow would begin to melt and they had some hope of walking out. It was up to them: live or die.

There were ten bodies frozen in the cemetery. If they refrained from eating relatives —Parrado's mother and sister, the Methols' nephew, Francisco Abal—that left seven. The seven bodies would provide enough protein to sustain the twenty-six survivors for at least a month, perhaps longer. By that time, surely, the snow would have melted. It *had* to melt. The altimeter showed only 7,000 feet. They were *not* in the heart of the Andes, the land of eternal snow, but in the foothills. When the snow melted, the strongest could walk out and bring help for those who had to be left behind.

Another boy took up the case. In a sense, he said, they were lucky, very lucky, that some friends had died in the crash and there were ten bodies in the cemetery. What if nobody had been killed? In the final stages of starvation, wouldn't some turn instinctively to cannibalism, murdering for food? It would not be murder, not be immoral to eat those in the cemetery. They were already dead. Their spirits had departed, taken away by God. Perhaps God took them so that those left could survive until a way out could be found. The dead would not know. In death, they could help their friends to go on living, the supreme gift. Wouldn't they feel the

The Old Christinas Rugby Team, young, in top condition, before the fated trip.

Front and side views of the Fairchild F-227's shattered fuselage, the survivors' refuge for 70 days, as found by the rescue team.

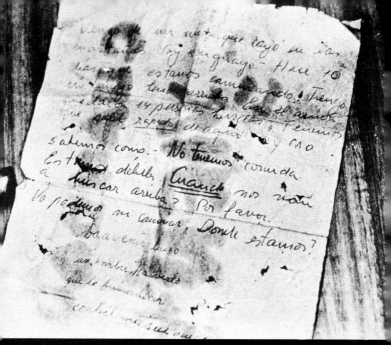

The note Parrado and Canessa threw across the river to Sergio Catalan telling of the survivors.

Fernando Parrado, Roberto Canessa and Sergio Catalan, the cowboy.

Canessa and Parrado, safe at Los Maitenes after their 10 day hike from the crash site.

The hero returned, Parrado embracing his friends.
A survivor arriving at the Santiago hospital.

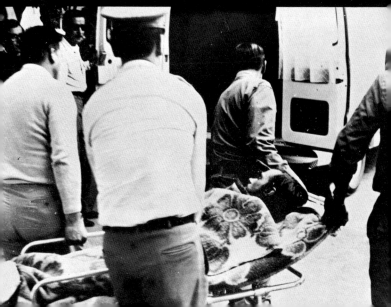

Carlos Paez in an emotional homecoming.
The survivors arrive safely back in Montevideo.

same way about it if they were alive and we were dead?

And so the decision was reached.

* * *

The turn to cannibalism—or in the more dignified Greek term, anthropophagy—was neither so rare nor so barbaric as some of the boys believed. Throughout the history of man, anthropophagy has been practiced willingly by many, and unwillingly by many more caught in extreme circumstances.

From earliest times, primitive tribes have willingly engaged in cannibalism. Usually the eating of human flesh was ritualized: warriors, for example, ate the dead of a competing tribe after battle. Some tribes believed that eating enemies killed in battle gave their own warriors a sort of superstrength that would pay dividends in future battles. Others, such as the Ojibwa Indians of North America, merely fell into the habit, finding human flesh a rare and delicate treat, superior to bison and other wild beasts. The Caribs, one of the primitive tribes discovered by the Spanish in the West Indies, gave the word cannibal to the language—"cannibal" being a corruption of the Spanish word for the Caribs.

In 1972, there were still many primitive tribes on earth willingly practicing cannibalism. They were located in the interior regions of New Guinea, west and central Africa, near the headwaters of the Amazon River in Latin America, Melanesia (especially the island of Fiji), Polynesia, Sumatra, Australia and New Zealand. The most notorious were the Maori tribes in New Zealand and the Batak tribes in Sumatra.

The recorded history of man is full of tales of anthropophagy practiced unwillingly, usually when under siege in war, or during prolonged famines. Under extreme circumstances, the Bible condones it. In Deuteronomy XXVIII, it is written: "And thou shalt eat the fruit of thine own body, the flesh of thy sons and of thy daughters . . . in siege and in the straitness."

In the old days, when famines ravished Europe, the starving killed wives, husbands, children and devoured them. They snatched corpses from gallows and fresh graves, or waylaid passers-by. In France, during the famine of 1030–32, one man consumed 48 humans. The flesh of humans was sold openly in the marketplace. In Russia, during the protracted famine of 1918–22, following the Communist takeover, there were countless recorded instances of cannibalism. The Russians resorted to it again in 1942, during the siege of Stalingrad.

The most famous instance of anthropophagy, and the best-documented, occurred in

the United States in the 1840s to a group
of pioneers, later to become known as the
Donner Party. Their story—their circumstances—closely paralleled that of the Old
Christians.

The Donner Party was a group of 87 men,
women and children who were bound for
California in 1846 in covered wagons. The
party was led by two brothers, George and
Jacob Donner, from Springfield, Illinois. At
the suggestion of a scout, the Donner Party
deviated from the usual route and went by
way of Salt Lake, then west to Lake Tahoe,
California, where there was said to be an
easy pass over the final mountain range, the
Sierra Nevadas. En route, the party encountered terrible hardships in the uncharted
mountains and deserts, losing oxen, wagons
and food. By the time they reached the
Sierra Nevadas, it was late in the year—
October. Unseasonable snows that would
make it one of the worst winters on record
had begun to fall. They couldn't get through
the pass.

The Donner Party camped on the east side
of the pass, near Lake Tahoe, building crude
cabins of timber and cowhides and tents.
They hoped to use the cabins as a staging
base for crossing the pass—when and if the
snow melted. The snow did not melt. On the
contrary, it piled up, ever deeper. The Party
had plenty of firewood and warm clothing,

but little food. In the first weeks most of the oxen, already near starvation, were killed and eaten.

When it was apparent that the food was running out and the snow was not going to melt, the Party sent several expeditions to climb the pass and seek help on the other side. Most turned back, but one, a large expedition of seventeen (five women, twelve men) that left on December 16 kept going. They slogged uphill on crude, homemade snowshoes, blinded by the snow. Near the top, they were caught in a blizzard and had to stop, taking shelter beneath blankets. They soon ran out of food. Some died. Those who survived ate the flesh of the dead, taking care not to eat a member of his own family. After 33 days, the remnants of this expedition, seven people, made it through the pass and into California. The women proved to be hardier than the men: all five of the women who started out made it; only two of the twelve men survived.

The seven who got across organized expeditions to go in and rescue the people left behind in the cabins. All this took much time. Most of the rescue expeditions failed. It was difficult to find volunteers to replace them. Little by little, the people in the cabins, including Jacob Donner, died of starvation. Many who lived—weak and apathetic—ate the dead.

When the rescue parties finally reached the cabins, they were appalled. Mrs. Jacob Donner had refused to eat her husband's body and was nearly dead herself, but she had cut it up to feed to her children. The rescuers found the children eating his heart and liver. The body was mutilated beyond recognition: the head had been decapitated and preserved in snow; the arms and legs were gone, the torso was cut open and the insides had been removed. They found hair, bones and half-eaten limbs around the fireplace. In another cabin, they found a group of adults who had eaten the children who had died. They were then preparing to eat an old woman. Her heart and liver and pieces of flesh were cooking in a pot. In another cabin, a man—obviously insane—told rescuers that the woman he had just eaten was the best meat he had ever tasted.

In all, 47 of the original Donner Party of 87 made it to California. They left no precise record of the number of human beings eaten, but authorities later estimated ten to fifteen. The survivors who ate human flesh were at first condemned by society for violating this taboo. But the Catholic theologians —there were several Catholics in the Donner Party—condoned their anthropophagy on the grounds that it was not a sin to eat the flesh of the dead to save one's own life. With the passing of time, the Donner Party regained respect. The site where they came to grief was named Donner Pass; a museum was erected in their memory.

* * *

The Old Christians had at least one considerable advantage over the Donner Party: ten bodies already dead in the cemetery. They did not have to prolong their own starvation until one of their friends or teammates died before they could eat. They could begin eating from a position of relative strength and with care *build* strength rather than see it ebb away. Yet there was one disadvantage: the boys had no firewood, no way to cook the meat.

It was the resourceful medical student Roberto Canessa who provided the solution. On his camping trips in Uruguay, he had frequently taken along dried beef, known as *charqui*—a specialty of the Indians of southern Brazil. (North American Indians called it jerky.) *Charqui* is made by placing raw meat in sunlight. After a few days, it dries out, becoming a tough, chewy substance rich in proteins and minerals. *Charqui* (or jerky) will keep indefinitely without refrigeration. In the old days, U.S. Indians and cowboys kept it in saddlebags for months.

Canessa began mass-producing *charqui* from human flesh. From the cemetery he disinterred the bodies of those least known to the Old Christians. He dismembered the bodies with the emergency ax. He carved out and threw away the "contaminated parts" (such as the intestines) and cut the remaining flesh with a razor into thin strips. He laid the strips on metal and erected reflectors to intensify the heat. The cooking process was enhanced by the thin air, which contained little oxygen. He utilized every edible portion of the human body, including heart, liver, kidneys, brains. The hands and feet which were tough and contained many bones and little meat were also discarded. The remains were buried in the snow.

All this was a laborious, not to say horrifying, process requiring many man-hours of hard labor. Canessa could not do it all by himself. Others pitched in, steeling themselves day by day, until the sight of a dismembered body no longer made them squeamish. In time, all who were able served as butchers and cooks.

The *charqui* was served twice a day. The boys called the people they ate "*compañeros*" —the Spanish word for "comrade." Most ate without hesitation, washing it down with water. A few, including Numa Turcatti, were revolted and could not keep it down. The other boys forced Turcatti to eat, to save his own life. But often Turcatti would throw away his share and go without.

The macabre menu was monotonous and

utterly lacking in taste appeal. But it was life-giving. Little by little, those who ate began to regain strength. The only real question was: would the food last until the snow melted?

CHAPTER SIXTEEN

Buried Alive

On the thirteenth day on the mountain, October 26, snow came again. It fell day after day, fine and soft, a powdery substance that would delight a skier. The snows curtailed all but the most essential activities. The 26 survivors jammed in a huddle inside the fuselage when it snowed, melted water and aired clothing when the sun came out.

But mostly they waited. For the snow to stop. For the weather to clear. For spring to come. For the snow to melt. For body strength to build.

One day merged with the next—a depressing tedium. The immense silence of the Andes preyed on them. They longed for the cacophony of the buses, taxis, trucks and cars on the Avenue 18th of July in downtown Montevideo. When someone became too depressed or apathetic and gave up all hope, the others converged on him, forming a group therapy session, drawing him out. Or they made feeble jokes. Carlos Páez declared that Donald Duck's rich uncle was sending a special plane from the States, equipped with all kinds of secret devices to find people marooned in the Andes. They decided, after a time, that Donald Duck's uncle had let them down.

One who continued to project remarkable cheerfulness was Rafael Echavarren, whose badly mangled right calf refused to heal. Although he was the most seriously injured and faced the probability of gangrene, he was fiercely independent. He insisted on crawling alone to the latrine which had been created outside near the nose of the plane. Once, when someone accidentally stepped on his leg, Echavarren involuntarily screamed. When he could speak again, he apologized. At night, when Daniel Fernandez massaged his leg to keep it from freezing, he would say gratefully: "If I live through this I'll send you cheese from my dairy farm for the rest of your life."

There was another problem. They were consuming food at a faster rate than anticipated: one body about every three days. The arithmetic made it clear that they could not wait forty days for the snow to melt. If they waited that long, there would be no food for those who tried to walk out and no food for those who remained behind. Thus the boys began to make plans for a big expedition: ten of the strongest would try to walk out. The sixteen weaker and injured ones, plus the woman, Liliana Methol, would remain behind.

The sixteenth day in the mountains, October 29, was clear. The boys went outside the plane, sunned the blankets and clothes, peeled off shirts and sat in the seats arranged along the outside of the fuselage, like park benches. Numa Turcatti, still refusing to eat very much, was happy for two reasons. He had found his older brother's camera, lost in the crash, and the next day, October 30, would be his 25th birthday. In spite of all, he had lived to celebrate it.

At about 6:00, after the sun dropped behind the mountains, the boys went inside the plane. They ate and prayed, then prepared to bed down, arranging the foam rubber cushions on the floor, stowing clothes in the port side luggage rack which, on account of the tilt of the plane to the right, was almost overhead. Some took off their shoes, preferring to sleep in two or three pairs of socks rather than shove a shoe in somebody's face.

Two boys, Diego Storm and Gustavo Nicolich, were depressed that night. Their good friend Roy Harley did all he could to cheer them up and make them comfortable. Usually Harley slept forward of Storm. That night he decided to switch places, to give Storm room to stretch out. Harley would sleep curled up, next to Nicolich. While this was going on, the others burrowed under the poncho-blankets, dozing off. Before closing his eyes, Fernando Parrado glanced at his watch. It was 7:10 p.m.

A second or two later—while Roy Harley was still standing—those who were awake heard two loud cracks. It was a terrifying sound, like lightning, or pistol shots. Then tons of soft snow smashed through the feeble barricade closing off the rear of the fuselage and flooded the cabin. The crack of lightning had touched off an avalanche of new snow. It rushed down the trough that the fuselage had ploughed when it slid down the mountain after the crash.

All the boys except Roy Harley were instantly buried alive under five feet of snow. It smashed them against the sides of the fuselage like a giant hand, knocking the breath from their lungs. In total panic, they fought, clawed, tried to get a footing to shove upwards for air, not knowing whether the snow was two feet deep or ten. The snow felt like a blanket of white lead, weighing tons. Many exhausted themselves in seconds and gave up.

One who did not was Fernando Parrado. Once he had read a magazine article about some people caught in an avalanche in Switzerland. He remembered that some had saved themselves by working their arms and hands to their faces, then pushing back the snow, forming an air pocket. Parrado did this, then began to shout for help.

Others did likewise. Roy Harley, buried chest deep, could hear their muffled voices beneath the snow. He began digging for his best friend Diego Storm, with whom he had just changed places. At that altitude, it was exhausting work. His bare hands lost all feeling in the freezing snow. He could not find Storm, but he saw a hand. He grabbed it and pulled. The face of Adolfo Strauch broke through the snow.

"Dig! Dig!" Harley shouted.

José Inciarte, who was certain that he was dying, prayed and clawed the snow away from his nose and mouth. As he struggled, he involuntarily urinated. Then he gave up. The weight of snow was too great. He closed his eyes to sleep, a sleep of death. Then he felt hands clawing at the snow around his head. Then fresh air.

It was Roy Harley. Harley pulled Inciarte from the snow then cried again:

"Dig! Dig!"

Carlos Páez was almost asleep when the avalanche struck. Like Parrado, he pushed the snow back from his face. Then he found a place to brace his feet. He shoved with all his might. His head broke through the snow. Roy Harley saw him and dragged him out.

Harley, Adolfo Strauch, Inciarte and Páez dug desperately toward the sound of voices, uncovering faces so the boys could breathe. Páez found Francois. Then, one by one, the boys, pausing to warm their hands with cigarette lighters, uncovered Daniel Fernandez, Alvaro Mangino, Alfredo Delgado, Rafael

157

Echavarren, Numa Turcatti, Javier Methol, Roberto Canessa, Eduardo Strauch, Arturo Nogueira, José Pedro Algorta, Antonio Vizintín, Gustavo Zerbino, Ramon Sabella.

They found the others, too, but they were dead: Diego Storm and Gustavo Nicolich; the team captain, Marcelo Perez; the mechanic, Carlos Roque; Daniel Maspons, a hero of the first expedition to the top of the mountain; "the Brute," Enrique Platero, who had survived being impaled by an aluminum rod in the crash. Finally, Liliana Methol, the fifth and last woman to die.

The boys, cold, wet, freezing and nearly dead from exhaustion, tried mouth-to-mouth resuscitation. It was too late. There were seven more bodies for the cemetery.

Then they remembered Fernando Parrado. Where was he? Again, frantic digging. At last they found and uncovered his head. Parrado had been buried fifteen or twenty minutes when they found him. He was still alive. They dug him out, believing that for the second time, God had worked a miracle. Parrado, having been "born twice" on the mountain, was more convinced than ever that God had spared him for a special reason.

Counting Parrado, there were nineteen survivors. They pulled extra clothing from the luggage rack. Those who were without shoes, wrapped their feet. They huddled together and against the dead bodies to keep warm.

They talked all night to stay awake, lying on top of the snow, breathing on one another, massaging limbs, praying for the dead and themselves.

When the sun came up on October 30, a faint light filtered through the snow-covered windows. It shone on a bizarre scene: nineteen shivering, wet survivors and seven bodies, lying atop the snow inside the cabin. The survivors were too cold and exhausted to dig themselves out. As they lay there, on Turcatti's birthday, a second, smaller avalanche descended upon the fuselage, piling up more snow.

For some, the shock of the avalanche was more severe than the crash itself. Javier Methol, who lost his wife, was severely affected. Up to then, his contribution to survival had been significant. After the avalanche, he drew apart from the group, remaining huddled with his wife's body. His strength ebbed; he fell into a state of apathy.

Carlos Páez, Roy Harley and Roberto Francois had lost their best friends, two members of "the gang," Diego Storm and Gustavo Nicolich. It was a mind-numbing blow. "The gang" (which included Gilberto Regules) had all survived the crash. Only Echavarren had been badly hurt. Now two were gone. How many more would go?

During that day, some of the boys slept fitfully, occasionally waking up screaming that another avalanche was boiling down upon them. All were despairing, apathetic or terrified. Their home had been wrecked. The work teams so carefully organized had been decimated. What new horrors lay ahead? How much shock could the human mind, however young and resilient, sustain? Would they all go insane?

That night, after the sun went down, the cold set in again. The nineteen who lived huddled together, massaging, talking, struggling to avoid sleep from which they might not awaken. At midnight, October 31, Carlos Páez had a birthday, his nineteenth. They sang happy birthday in English to him. One boy remembered that it would also have been the birthday of the bank clerk Julio Martinez-Lamas, who died in the crash. They prayed for his soul.

When the sun came up on Tuesday, October 31, a few of the boys had strength and climbing spirits. During prayers, they tried to encourage the dispirited, the many who were ready to give up and die. The spark spread, slowly, and soon they were discussing how to tunnel out of the cabin, clean it out, bury the dead.

The first step was the tunnel. They dug by hand, taking turns. The medical student, Gustavo Zerbino, dug so hard he injured his fingers; they would remain impaired for months. After hours of exhausting work, they broke through to the outside. One by one they crawled through the tunnel "like babies," drinking up the sunshine, staring into the bright, silent landscape that they hated, the wall of mountain that formed their deadly prison.

The second step was to bury the dead. They dragged the seven rigid bodies from the fuselage and to the cemetery, where they were buried with appropriate prayer. Then they turned to the monumental task of cleaning the snow from the cabin and reerecting a stronger barricade at the rear. With only a dozen boys capable of hard work, and many of these dispirited, it took a long while. When it was done, November 1st, the boys celebrated Alfredo Delgado's 25th birthday.

There was one important offshoot of the avalanche: a dramatic change in the food arithmetic. It cut by seven the number to be fed and raised by six the number of bodies in the cemetery that could be eaten. (At the request—or demand—of Javier Methol, his wife's body was placed on the excluded list along with the other relatives—his nephew, Francisco Abal, and Eugenia and Susana Parrado.) The six extra bodies, in effect, guaranteed a longer period of survival, provided they were not all wiped out by another avalanche.

CHAPTER SEVENTEEN

Lost Cause at the Tail Section

In the early days of November, following the avalanche, the weather did not improve as the boys hoped it might. There were snowstorms that forced them to huddle inside the freezing fuselage for days. Fearing another avalanche, they slept with their hearts in their mouths. Whenever they heard an unusual noise, they scrambled madly out of their "house."

Time dragged. An hour sometimes seemed to last a week. Their vision narrowed to a single level of consciousness: survival. They did only what was necessary to stay alive. They ate. They melted snow for water. They prayed earnestly and incessantly. They encouraged the dispirited. They cursed the snow and the mountains, the Uruguayan Air Force and those who had given them up for lost and called off the search. Some, losing control, screamed in anger and despair.

Of the nineteen survivors, nearly one-third were down—or out. Three still had serious leg injuries: Mangino, Delgado, Echavarren. Delgado and Mangino were improving, but Mangino's leg had not set properly and he could only crawl. Nogueira was still mentally unstable. Javier Methol was still in shock following the death of his wife. Numa Turcatti, who refused to eat, grew weaker.

In mid-November, another boy, José Luis Inciarte, joined the sick list. During one night, when the boys were huddled close, the circulation in both his legs was cut off. When he awoke, his ankles were swollen "like footballs." In subsequent days, lumps "the size of tennis balls" appeared on his legs. Inciarte sterilized a razor blade and lanced the lumps. Pus gushed out. After that, Inciarte could not walk.

Some of the boys grew stronger. Among these were Roberto Canessa, Antonio Vizintín, Fernando Parrado, Eduardo and Adolfo Strauch, Daniel Fernandez, Roy Harley, Carlos Páez. They did the heavy work: making food, repairing the fuselage, airing the blankets, caring for the injured. They also talked endlessly about escape: planning an expedition they would send to the outside world.

After the middle of November, the weather improved. Spring came to the Andes. It stopped snowing. The temperature rose. The snow that had accumulated on the mountainside began to melt. They could measure the rate of melting by watching the level of snow against the fuselage. It dropped a foot, then two. The snow that remained compressed itself into a relatively firm mass: soft and mushy in daytime, solid ice at night.

As the snow melted, the bodies in the cemetery and the remains of those who had been consumed were exposed. To preserve the food supply, it was necessary to rebury the dead every few days, an exhausting and depressing task. At first, the boys also reburied the remains. But they soon saw this was an extravagant expenditure of energy. After that, they left the remains exposed They grew used to the sight.

As the days dragged on, there were many high and lows. On November 23rd, they celebrated Roberto Francois' 21st birthday. Later Arturo Nogueira, who had not been well since the crash, developed problems in his legs. Canessa did all he could, but Nogueira did not respond. One night he died in his sleep. The next day they buried him in the cemetery. He was the twenty-seventh to die.

Then Rafael Echavarren, who had been so cheerfully resolute all these weeks, got gangrene in his leg wound. Knowing that he was dying, Echavarren made a will. His Land Rover, he said, should be given to his girl-friend, Anita Lawlor; his motorcycle to the foreman at the farm, Walter Aguerre, who had helped him start the dairy plant. He sent a message to his parents and to Anita: "If I don't return, do not be sad, don't mourn. Anita, please do not be a grieving old woman: get married." He added a final plea: "Please tell my father not to abandon my body in the Andes."

Canessa considered amputating Echavarren's leg. But then he seemed to get better. Carlos Páez was determined to *will* Echavarren back to health. He attended to his needs, sat by him, constantly encouraging Echavarren to pray. Then, one day, Echavarren became delirious. He remained that way for three days. On the third day, Carlos heard a death rattle. He gave Echavarren mouth-to-mouth resuscitation until he himself was exhausted. Then Echavarren died and was removed to the cemetery.

The older boys, who had become the leaders of the group, now finalized plans for the expedition to the outside world. For this dangerous—perhaps fatal—mission, they chose three, those considered the strongest and best qualified in hiking: Fernando Parrado, Roberto Canessa and Antonio Vizintín. They conferred on these three the status of superwarriors, giving them extra rations for two weeks and a more comfortable place to sleep. The three made sleeping bags and some nights they slept outside the fuselage, as a drill. During the day, they did special exercises and made short excursions from the plane to gain experience in traveling on the snow. They studied the maps and the terrain, memorizing the surrounding mountains and ridges so that if they did reach civilization, they could lead a rescue party back to the right place.

In late November the three boys made one

or two false starts, seeking the best way out. On the second of these, by accident, they made a startling find: the tail section of the aircraft, *downhill* from the fuselage. They found the galley, the luggage compartment brimming with suitcases, many cartons of cigarettes (presents from the Abal cigarette factory to the Chilean hosts), the two nickel-cadmium batteries and one body: Juan Carlos Menendez, who had been among the eight missing.

The most important items in the tail section were the two batteries. Before he died in the avalanche, the mechanic, Roque, had told the boys the batteries could be used to operate the radio transmitter. If this worked, they could transmit a call for help and cancel plans for the dangerous expedition.

The boys removed the batteries from the lower tail section. They were heavy: about 40 to 50 pounds each. Each felt as though it weighed 150 pounds. They put the batteries on a sled fashioned from the luggage compartment door. Then they started uphill for the fuselage, tugging, pushing, stumbling, falling. Quite soon they were exhausted. The task was beyond them.

What to do? There was one solution: bring more manpower. They divided forces. Roberto Canessa remained at the tail section. Parrado and Vizintín returned to the fuselage to get help.

The new hope for salvation now shifted to the person of Roy Harley, the electronics buff who had saved them in the avalanche. It was all up to Harley. Did he have the know-how? He would try.

During these discussions, someone made a proposal. Why struggle *uphill* with the batteries? Why not remove the radio from the fuselage and tow it downhill to the tail section?

That made sense. Using the heavy emergency ax, Roy Harley and others chopped the radio controls from the cockpit (including the ADF and VOR) and then hacked the "black boxes" from a panel behind the cockpit. They gathered up extra wire from the fuselage, the plane's radio antenna, and loaded everything on a sled made from seat backs.

Many boys joined the return trek to the tail: Carlos Páez, Daniel Fernandez, Gustavo Zerbino. They went down the mountain in high spirits, towing the sled and its precious cargo. Roberto Canessa, the first boy to spend a night away from the fuselage alone, gave them a warm greeting. In the interim, he had found the medicine chest.

Roy Harley set to work without delay. He tested the batteries. They had power. Then he began connecting wires. The other boys gathered around watching, hoping, praying.

Roque may have had his judgment seriously impaired in the crash. Or perhaps he knew nothing about the electrical system on the Fairchild. In any case, his suggestion that the battery could operate the radio transmitter was unfortunate. The radio transmitter operated on 110 volts AC from a generator on the main engine. The battery was 28 volts DC. The only way to convert the 28-volt DC battery to a 110-volt AC current was to build a small motor-generator that would operate off the battery and produce 110-volt AC current. Even if Harley had had the know-how to manufacture such a device, there were no tools or equipment to do it. "It would have required an electronics specialist," a U.S. engineer said. "And he would have to have had a complete laboratory."

Roy Harley went on connecting wires. They heard a humming sound—the radio was warming up! Harley connected another wire. They heard an ominous noise. Some tubes had blown. The humming stopped. Harley tried going at it another way. And another. After hours and hours of experimenting, the boys realized the game was lost. They had been chasing fool's gold. They would have to return to the plan of sending out Parrado, Canessa and Vizintín.

This large expedition remained at the tail section for several days, fooling with the radio and batteries, searching the luggage, foraging for other goodies. Daniel Fernandez found his I.D. papers. Some of the suitcases yielded bottles of whiskey and cognac. These, and some items of clothing (sweaters, jackets) were loaded on the sled for the return to the fuselage.

Looking at all the luggage, which was too heavy to take back up the hill, one of the boys had an idea: why not use it to make a cross that could be seen from the air? If Parrado, Canessa and Vizintín reached civilization, and returned by airplane, it might help them re-locate the area.

The idea won immediate approval. They picked a site, broke up the luggage and laid it—and some clothing—out in the form of a cross. To keep it from blowing away, they dug shallow trenches and embedded it in the snow.

Before they left, they wrote out a note and left it at the tail section in case rescuers found that part: "There are 17 survivors in the fuselage which is higher up in this same valley. Situation desperate." It was dated December 7 and was signed by Fernando Parrado, Roberto Canessa, Roy Harley and Antonio Vizintín.

All this had been hard work. On the way back to the fuselage, Roy Harley and Carlos Páez gave out. Páez wanted to lie down in the snow and go to sleep. Harley forced him to go on. Then Harley collapsed and Páez

169

and others had to help *him*. After this excursion, Harley and Páez went on the sick list and were not able to leave the fuselage again.

The discovery of the tail section, and the subsequent work there, drained Parrado, Canessa and Vizintín of vital energy and food supplies. Before setting off again, they had to rebuild strength and prepare more food. Their departure date was postponed. By that time—they all hoped—the snow would have melted further and the trek would be easier.

CHAPTER EIGHTEEN

A Green Valley to the West?

After the futile expedition to the tail, some of the boys again fell into deep despair. Having slogged through the snow that short distance and returned, they doubted that the expedition could ever get out of the mountains. Some believed they were all destined to die in this hellhole, one by one.

Numa Turcatti, who still refused to eat, had almost turned into a skeleton. The boys tried repeatedly to force him to eat, but Turcatti would not comply. He continued to throw his food away. He clung to life day after day, but his death seemed inevitable. One day, someone accidently stepped on his ankle. The skin died and gangrene set in. Canessa gave him antibiotics, but Turcatti was too weak to fight off an infection. One morning they found him dead. He was the twenty-ninth, and last, to die, leaving sixteen survivors.

After Turcatti died, the most seriously ill was Roy Harley. The expedition to the tail had broken his health. He went steadily downhill, losing all appetite. Canessa gave him antibiotics but Harley lost weight rapidly. Soon he was skeletal, like Turcatti had been and, like many, suffering from scurvy. It seemed a miracle that he lived at all.

By the time Turcatti died, the three boys who were to leave for the outside world, Parrado, who celebrated his 23rd birthday on December 9th, Canessa and Vizintín, had recovered strength. They might have waited even longer for the snow to melt, but the sight of Roy Harley going downhill gave them a powerful motive to leave. Roy Harley had saved them in the avalanche. They felt they owed it to Harley to try to reach civilization in time to save his life.

On the morning of December 12, the three boys got up at 3:00 a.m. They packed food for fifteen days, a bottle of water and a bottle of whiskey in handmade knapsacks. The other boys donated their warmest and best clothing: trousers, sweaters, windbreakers, socks. Each of the three put on several pairs of trousers and two or three sweaters, a jacket and rugby shoes. They wore sunglasses made by Adolfo Strauch, snowshoes made from seat cushions and carried walking sticks made from aluminum tubing. Each had a sleeping bag made from the plastic insulation they found on the cabin heating ducts. Parrado carried the plane's compass.

Before they set off, all the boys prayed a rosary, asking God to give them a safe journey. Afterwards, Parrado remembered the red slippers he had bought in Mendoza for his nephew. He put one in his pocket for a good luck charm and gave the other to Alfredo Delgado, telling him to bring it out when he was rescued. To all, Parrado said: "Boys, I promise we will have you out of here before Christmas."

The three boys buckled into safety lines made of seatbelts. At 4:00 a.m. they left the fuselage, walking west, toward a range of mountains. The snow was still frozen hard. They made good time until the sun came up and turned the snow soft and mushy. Afterwards, they slogged on, supported by the snowshoes and walking poles.

The initial objective was to climb the mountain to the west. They believed that when they made it to the top, they would find green on the other side: the foothills of the Andes. After that, it would be easier going, ten miles downhill to civilization. For this reason, they pushed as hard as possible until they got to the top of the mountain.

They vastly underestimated the time it would take to scale the mountain. Every foot of the way was agony. First freezing winds howled across the slope. Then the sun came out bringing blazing heat. Each step took them higher, into thinner air where it became difficult to breathe. Every few steps they had to stop to catch their breath.

The boys at the fuselage could see them, tiny black specks inching up the vast white carpet. They prayed them on, shouting encouragement.

After twelve hours, the boys on the mountain gave out, having gone only one-third of the planned distance. They had to camp where they were on the open slope. They dug a hole in the snow and placed the sleeping bags inside, pegging them down with the aluminum poles so they wouldn't slide downhill. They used the cushions of the snowshoes for pillows. All night, they huddled together to keep warm.

The second day was a repetition of the first. They climbed ever higher, slipping, falling, cursing the Andes, the endless wet snow. Each fall was a small drama. There was no turning back. If someone got injured—sprained an ankle—he would have to be left behind. That had been the agreement. The boys at the fuselage followed their slow progress with growing concern.

On the third day, Parrado, who never seemed to tire, forged ahead and reached the top of the mountain. The view was awesome—and demoralizing. As far as he could see (he was nearsighted), there were more snowcapped mountains. There was no sign of green or the foothills in the west. One fact was immediately clear: they were much deeper in the Andes than they had believed. To get out would take much longer—and much more food—than they had planned.

Parrado returned to the place where Canessa and Vizintín had stopped, bringing the bad news. They discussed what they should do. Press on? Go back to the plane? Parrado would not entertain the idea of turning back. They *had* to go on. The only solution was to take the food of one man and send him back to the fuselage. They decided that Vizintín, the least strong of the three, should go back. Parrado and Canessa divided his food and told him to tell the others that the expedition would take much longer, perhaps four weeks. If they failed and further expeditions were necessary, they should take much more food with them.

The three bid each other farewell. Vizintín plopped down and glissaded down the mountain. In thirty minutes, he descended the slope that had taken them three days to climb. That same day, he returned to the fuselage carrying the bad news.

Parrado and Canessa continued climbing. Nearby they saw a higher peak. They climbed toward it, hoping for a better view of the topography. That night, they camped beneath a rock outcropping, discarding one of the sleeping bags, doubling up for warmth. The next day they climbed still higher, slipping, falling, ever fearful of starting an avalanche that would bury them.

At last they reached the top of the high peak. Canessa, with his superior eyesight, made a survey. Far in the west, on the distant horizon, he thought he saw a green valley. But between them and the valley—if it *was* a valley—there were endless mountains. If they had to climb each one, Canessa estimated, it would take them fifty days.

Standing on the peak, Canessa made another observation: he could see a river, he thought, winding through the mountains. If they could find the river, they might follow it down, avoiding the peaks. A river, eventually, would lead them into the foothills. They pushed on, crossing a frozen lake.

* * *

Back at the fuselage, the fourteen boys left behind were less than overjoyed by the news Vizintín brought back. If it had taken Parrado and Canessa three days to climb one mountain and there were countless more mountains to climb, how many weeks would it take them to get out? Could they get out at all? *Why* were there countless mountains to the west? How deep in the Andes were they? Perhaps they should consider an expedition to the east?

These questions led to another: how long would the food supply hold out? The arithmetic had changed again. Nogueira, Echavarren and Turcatti were dead; Parrado and Canessa were gone; poor Roy Harley ate practically nothing. However, there were still fourteen boys to feed. If they continued to exclude the bodies of Francisco Abal, Eugenia and Susana Parrado, Liliana Methol and those who had died of gangrene, the food would not last long. If they sent out another expedition (to the east or west) those chosen to go would need double rations to build strength, then a large supply of food to take with them.

All these considerations set off a new hunt for the missing bodies. There was one at the tail, they knew, and Carlos Valeta was just up the hill. But where were the other six?

The strongest of the fourteen—the Strauches and Zerbino—began searching uphill. They found the body of Carlos Valeta and brought it to the cemetery. Later they found the body of Daniel Shaw farther uphill. His friends brought his body down on a sled in two stages, half the distance the first day, half the second.

The boys assumed correctly that the last five of the missing bodies were uphill from the place they found Shaw. They left them there for the time being. It was too difficult a climb to retrieve them: there was the ever-present danger of starting an avalanche. It was colder up there and the snow was deeper. The bodies would be well preserved until they were needed.

CHAPTER NINETEEN

A Cross in the Snow

As the days passed into weeks, the weeks into months, most of the parents, relatives and friends of the Old Christians gave up hope. The Stella Maris School conducted a Requiem Mass. But a few parents, encouraged by the visions of the Dutch seer Gerard Croiset, or by faith in a religious miracle, refused to concede. Rafael Echavarren's father went to Chile and conducted an expedition into the mountains near Talca. The mother of Carlos Páez, Madelon Rodriguez, rode a horse up into the mountains until the snow covered her stirrups.

The artist Carlos Páez Vilaró had not given up either. He spent November in Chile, ringing doorbells, flying over the mountains in small planes. He organized land expeditions. He persuaded several of the fathers to put up money to rent a helicopter.

In early December, when the snow began to melt in the Andes, Vilaró was more hopeful than ever. He returned to Montevideo and organized a group of fathers who in turn petitioned the Uruguayan Air Force for a helicopter. It was not the most favorable time for such a request. Uruguay, like Chile,

was being rocked by new political upheaval.
The Uruguayan Army (allied with the Air
Force) claimed it had discovered widespread
corruption in the Bordaberry government.
Some high government officials had secretly
sold 20 percent of the Uruguayan gold reserves abroad. The economy was in danger
of total collapse; inflation had increased in
the year 1972 by almost 100 percent. For the
first time in the twentieth century, the Uruguayan military was overtly flexing its muscles and threatening to take over the government. The few Uruguayan Air Force helicopters were needed at home for the impending crisis.

But Vilaró was not to be denied. The head
of the Air Force, Brigadier General Jose Perez
Caldas, agreed to furnish not a helicopter but
a fixed-wing aircraft. What they got was an
ancient, beat-up, twin-engine DC-3 (or by
military designation, C-47), number 508, obtained from the United States years before.
The fathers could have it for ten days.

On Sunday, December 10, the expedition
formed up at Montevideo's Carrasco airport.
It included Carlos Páez Vilaró, Roy Harley,
Sr., Gustavo Nicolich, Sr., Dr. Juan Carlos
Canessa and the Pluna pilot, Raul Rodriguez,
who was an uncle of Madelon Rodriguez and
a lifelong friend of Nicolich and Canessa.
The pilots of the C-47, Major Terra and Lt.
Lepere, were volunteers, close friends of the

Fairchild pilots, Ferradas and Lagurara. In addition, there was a helicopter pilot on board to learn how to fly search and rescue missions.

The old plane shook and vibrated down the runway and lifted into the air. It lumbered west, up the Rio de la Plata, toward Buenos Aires. Fifteen minutes after take-off, the left engine ran rough. Then it gave off a noisy "bang." The pilot feathered the prop and made an emergency landing at Palomar airport, Buenos Aires. When the mechanic pulled off the engine cowling, he found a broken connecting rod. The pilot, Major Terra, confided to Raul Rodriguez that the plane had had four engine failures—and four emergency landings—in the past two weeks.

The fathers were angry that the Uruguayan Air Force had given them a worthless and dangerous crate. They might well have given up then and there. However, they hoped the presence of a Uruguayan plane in Chile—any Uruguayan plane—would spur SAR to renew the search. They proceeded to Santiago by commercial jet to make advance plans, while Terra called Montevideo for a new engine for the C-47.

On arrival in Santiago, the fathers went immediately to SAR. Major Ivanovic received them cordially, and gave them all the technical information he possessed. However, Ivanovic was of the opinion that until more snow melted, a renewed SAR search would prove fruitless. He held out little hope that anyone in the Fairchild might be alive.

The pilot Raul Rodriguez studied the technical information. He attributed the cause of the crash to the eighteen-minute delay in takeoff from Mendoza. "I believe he calculated all his reporting points in advance," Rodriguez said later, "and got mixed up in his paperwork en route, going by the original plan which called for a 2:00 p.m. takeoff."

Carlos Páez Vilaró, still under the influence of the Dutch seer, wanted to focus the C-47 search near Talca, where the seer said they would find the wreck. But after studying all the information, Rodriguez concluded the plane could not possibly have crashed there. He agreed with the 20-mile-square search area near Tinguiririca that SAR had originally fixed. Nicolich, Canessa and Roy Harley voted for the same area.

While waiting for the C-47 to arrive, Páez Vilaró called on a pilot friend who had flown him over the Andes before. On December 13, the pilot flew Vilaró and Rodriguez on a three-hour search mission near Tinguiririca in a Beechcraft Baron. Although Vilaró and Rodriquez must have flown right over Parrado and Canessa, they saw nothing.

That same day, the C-47 with its new engine set off for Santiago. It crossed the Andes safely, but when it was approaching Santiago, the new engine began to shake and run rough. Said Rodriguez: "It was crazy. It was the carburetor that was causing all the trouble. They put a new engine on, but left on the old carburetor." After landing at Santiago, Terra replaced the carburetor.

Vilaró and others had slight faith that the C-47 could carry out the mission. On December 14, they went off to look for a helicopter. On that day, the C-47 flew its first search mission with Rodriguez and Gustavo Nicolich in the rear cabin. The air was turbulent. The old plane bounced and shook dangerously. Even so, they spent two hours searching the area near Tinguiririca and El Palomo. They saw nothing.

The news of this Uruguayan search was broadcast by the radio station *Spectador* in Montevideo. The fourteen boys at the fuselage heard it on the morning broadcast and were wildly hopeful. They fashioned a second, larger cross near the fuselage by hollowing out a shallow trench in the snow with seat backs.

On Friday, December 15, the C-47 took off for its second search mission. All the fathers made this flight: Vilaró, Canessa, Nicolich, Harley. This time, they flew to the south of Tinguiririca.

Midway during the flight, Gustavo Nicolich, who had taken station at one of the windows, blinked his eyes and looked hard.

Then with unsuppressed excitement, he shouted: "We've found it! We've found it! Look. A cross!"

The others gathered at windows. Yes, it was true: a cross in the snow. The pilot circled, making a fix by radio. The men shouted for joy, slapping one another on the back. They asked the pilot to descend for a closer look, but he refused: it was no place to lose an engine.

The C-47 returned to Santiago. The fathers rushed to SAR. SAR alerted the mountain-climbing group, CSA. Nobody had heard anything about a cross. It had not been seen by the SAR search planes in October. It must have been made by the boys in the Fairchild after the October search. Major Ivanovic called the Argentine Air Force in Mendoza. They had no knowledge of a cross either.

The find raised a small but delicate international problem. The cross was located at 35 degrees 7 minutes south, 70-13 west. This was Argentine territory, where SAR had no responsibility, no legal right to search. Major Ivanovic called Mendoza and asked the Argentine Air Force for help. They agreed to send a reconnaissance plane the following day.

The news of this find spread like wildfire, relayed to Montevideo by ham radio operators and telephone. Soon after, the news was broadcast on Montevideo radio and television stations. The other parents, relatives and friends of the Old Christians were thunderstruck. Could the boys be alive? After more than two months in the cold snows of the Andes?

Gilberto Regules was up in the country changing a tire on his car when the news came over the radio. He listened in disbelief. Had all his friends—"the gang"—come back from the dead? It seemed inconceivable. In great excitement, Regules finished changing the tire, picked up a friend and raced hellbent for Montevideo.

The next day at the fuselage the boys heard the news on the morning news broadcast. It caused a frenzy of excitement, wild rejoicing and backslapping. All that day, those who could remained outside the fuselage, eyes on the sky. They had been found!

On Saturday, December 16, the C-47 took off again to help the Argentine reconnaissance plane. The two planes rendezvoused in the air near the cross. The C-47 circled high over the spot, the engine running rough again. The Argentine plane—a U.S. F-86 jet —swept down into the valley taking photographs. The Argentine pilot reported by radio to the C-47 that he saw the cross—and a radio antenna nearby.

Radio antenna? How could that be?

The mystery was cleared up hours later.

The Argentines reported the cross was not one made by the boys, but rather an observation post of the Department of Irrigation. Scientists had bored holes in the snow in the form of a cross in order to study the rate the snow melted. This information helped them design irrigation ditches to bring Andes water to the vineyards at Mendoza, Chilecito and Malargue.

This discouraging news was soon broadcast by Montevideo radio and television stations. The hopes raised were once again cruelly dashed. Gilberto Regules, making plans for a trip to Chile to rejoin his friends, canceled them with heavy heart. Once again he resigned himself to the reality: his friends were dead. When the boys at the fuselage heard the broadcast, they cried.

The C-47 search, it seemed, was turning into a comedy of errors. The engine was still running rough. The turbulence in the Andes was beginning to loosen crucial bolts in the wings and fuselage. The flights had not encouraged SAR to resume the search. They had wasted three days on the Argentine cross.

There was time for one more flight. They scheduled it for Sunday, December 17. Two senior CSA men joined the party: Claudio Lucero, a physical education teacher, and Osvaldo Villegas, a businessman. They flew to Tinguiririca, then toward the east. The air was turbulent, the C-47 bounced and shook, but Major Terra was determined to make the most of this last day. By chance, he banked the plane and descended into the valley where the Fairchild fuselage lay.

The boys heard the engines. They rushed outside and looked skyward, scarcely believing their eyes. The plane was there, in their valley, flying low. They waved and shouted frantically.

Major Terra flew close to the ground, passing over the fuselage at about 1,000 feet. He kept the plane very low, flying toward a peak, until the last possible second. Then he threw it into a steep climbing turn. Raul Rodriguez, who was sitting at a window in the rear of the cabin, was thrown violently upward. His head struck the overhead luggage rack and he suffered a deep cut over his eye. Nursing his wound, he damned the pilot for that maneuver.

The C-47 lifted over the peaks and climbed out. Terra turned south toward Planchon, then west to Curico, then north to Santiago. The boys at the fuselage watched the plane disappear toward the south, certain once again they had been found.

Amid the rejoicing, one boy sounded a somber note. Parrado and Canessa had been gone five full days. There had been no word on the news broadcasts to indicate they had found their way out. They were probably dead, lost in a crevasse or buried beneath an avalanche. Now the fourteen had been found and they would have to look for the two that had gone to save them. Few believed Parrado or Canessa would ever be found alive.

CHAPTER TWENTY

Converging Trails

Fernando Parrado and Roberto Canessa were not lost in a crevasse or buried by an avalanche. They were hiking westward. During the day, they walked, urged on by Parrado, who never seemed to want to stop for rest. At night, they huddled together in the sleeping bag.

They had many close calls. While descending a slope, both boys lost their footing. They slid down the mountainside on their backs at a speed that felt like one hundred miles an hour to Parrado. They lost the sleeping bag, the snowshoes, the knapsacks of food and other gear. But at the end of this slide, they found a river. It was the upper reaches of the Rio del Azufre, which flows to the west.

They followed the river south, scrambling over rocks, grateful for the strength of their rugby shoes. On Sunday, December 17, when the C-47 was flying over the boys at the fuselage, Parrado and Canessa saw the first rocks clear of snow. About then, Canessa collapsed. He was ill, could walk no further. Parrado told him: "We must walk or we will die."

But Canessa could not walk unassisted. Parrado, refusing to leave his buddy behind, put Canessa's arms over his shoulder and went on, thinking of Roy Harley. Later that day, they found the first sign of civilization: an empty food can, probably left by campers or cowboys. "You see," Parrado said, encouraging Canessa, "we are almost there."

Late in the afternoon of December 20, they saw a movement in the bushes and stopped to investigate. The nearsighted Parrado could not make out anything. Canessa said: "They're cows! They must belong to someone. There must be a farm nearby."

By then, both boys were famished. Canessa was too weak to move another step. Parrado laid Canessa on the ground, then conceived a plan. After dark, he would climb a tree and drop a large stone down and kill a cow. He would slaughter it and cook steaks. The plan seemed preposterous to Canessa, but he was too weak to object.

*   *   *

In Santiago the fathers who had come on the Uruguayan C-47 prepared to return to Montevideo. Páez Vilaró, who had decided to stay on in Chile for a few more days with the pilot Rodriguez, had a farewell dinner at the Hotel Crillon, to which he invited the owner of Tinguiririca, Joaquin Gandarillas. Gandarillas found the group in an unhappy mood, complaining about the C-47 and the futility of the search. Gandarillas did not encourage them; he believed by then there was no hope that anyone could be found alive. He advised the fathers to wait until midsummer, when all the snow melted. Perhaps then they might find the plane, recover the bodies and give them a Christian burial in Uruguay.

The C-47 set off for Monevideo via Curico and Planchon Pass. While going over Planchon, the engine that had given them so much trouble began running rough again. The pilot, Major Terra, had no choice: either keep it going or face the possibility of crashing in Planchon. In spite of vibration so severe he believed the engine might tear from its mounts, he kept it going. Gustavo Nicolich said later: "At that point, I didn't care anymore. I was prepared to die."

Major Terra nursed the engine until the C-47 cleared the Andes. Then he shut it down and radioed Malargue that he was coming in for an emergency landing. But Malargue said no: there was construction on the runway and the field was closed. Terra —flying on one engine—continued on to the closest field, San Rafael.

When Major Terra declared the emergency over Planchon, it was heard by radio hams and Santiago Control. Someone then flashed word to Montevideo, exaggerating and twisting the news: the C-47 was missing or had crashed in the Andes. When this news reached the wives of Dr. Canessa, Roy Harley and Gustavo Nicolich, they were beside themselves with new worry.

At San Rafael, the fathers split forces. Dr. Canessa had to leave for Montevideo: December 21 was his wedding anniversary and he had promised his wife he would be home to celebrate it. He left by bus for Buenos Aires, six hundred miles to the east. Roy Harley and Gustavo Nicolich remained with the C-47 out of loyalty to the crewmen who had risked their lives on more than one occasion during the search.

* * *

Páez Vilaró and Raul Rodriguez continued the search. They got in touch with the miner Camilo Figueroa, who claimed he had seen the Fairchild flying over Planchon on the day it was lost. They brought him to Santiago where Rodriguez interrogated him. Rodriguez believed his story, despite the technical errors (red plane, four engines, etc.). It fit Rodriguez' theory that the pilot had made an error and turned north too soon. The miner, Rodriguez believed, was more reliable than the Dutch seer.

Meanwhile, Vilaró talked his friend Fernando Madrones into making another flight in a small plane. They took along the miner and one of the senior CSA men, Claudio Lucero. They flew to Planchon, then turned north toward Tinguiririca. Madrones, a skilled Andes pilot, flew low and slow, avoiding severe turbulence. During one low pass over a hilltop, Lucero saw footprints in the snow —a trail about one hundred yards long. He shouted, calling attention to the trail. Madrones made another pass. Vilaró took pictures with his long-lens camera.

They pondered this strange discovery. Footprints here? Impossible, Lucero said. Yet they were clearly footprints. Vilaró was convinced they had been made by the boys. Lucero doubted. The footprints were fresh. His long experience in the Andes told him that no one in the Fairchild could be alive. The prints, he speculated, must have been made by some people of the area. Perhaps they knew the location of the crash and were going to loot it, rob the dead.

On the following day, December 20, Vilaró and Rodriguez were in San Fernando. They called on a Chilean Army colonel, Enrique Morel Donoso, who commanded the Colchagua Regiment, a unit of special mountain troops stationed there to defend Planchon Pass should any outside forces attempt to cross it. Colonel Morel, a rising star in the Chilean Army and a man with artistic taste, remembered Páez Vilaró from a visit to Uruguay in 1971. Colonel Morel had visited Vilaró's home, Casapueblo, in Punta del Este. He remembered meeting the son, Carlos.

Vilaró asked Colonel Morel for a helicopter so that he could inspect the footprints. Morel provided a helicopter, but talked Vilaró out of trying to relocate the footprints. Like Lucero, Morel doubted they had been made by the boys. How could anyone possibly be alive after two months? Better, Morel said, to use it to search southeast of Curico. Morel had met a man who said the plane had crashed in that area.

Vilaró probed: What man? Morel explained that it was a hitchhiker he had picked up one day weeks ago, a mountain man. Since the location fit with that of the Dutch seer, Vilaró was eager to try it.

It was a pleasant day for a helicopter flight: cloudless, no turbulence. They flew south to Curico, then into the passes in the foothills. They saw nothing. When they returned to San Fernando, Colonel Morel gave them dinner then sent them on to Santiago in the helicopter with a promise that he would make it available after Christmas. Vilaró and Rodriguez made plans to return to Montevideo by commercial jet.

* * *

That same night, Fernando Parrado and Roberto Canessa, lying by the River Azufre, built a fire—their first—and prepared to carry out Parrado's scheme to kill and slaughter a cow. At about 7:00 p.m., Canessa thought he saw a movement across the river. It looked like a man on horseback. He shouted to Parrado: "Look, is that a cowboy?"

Parrado looked. Yes, it was a man on horseback. He waved his walking poles and shouted. Canessa shouted. However, the river made too much noise. The cowboy could see but not hear them. Parrado knelt down like a beggar or a penitent, pleading for help.

The man on the other side of the river was not really a cowboy but a cattleman. He was Sergio Catalan, brother-in-law of Efrain Millan, who was the chief foreman for the Gandarillas family. It was Catalan's sister, the wife of Efrain Millan, to whom Vilaró and Joaquin Gandarillas had talked on October 20, when they traveled by car into the mountains.

Catalan was not certain who these strangers might be. Campers? Terrorists on the run? (The aluminum walking poles could be rifles.) He rode off, returning to his camp. He had dinner with his sons. They talked about the strangers. They recalled the visit of Vilaró and Gandarillas, the story of the Uruguayan airplane crash. But that had been two months ago. No man could have survived in the mountains that long without food. Still. . . .

The following morning, December 21, Catalan gathered up four small loaves of bread, four pieces of cheese and returned to the place where he had seen the strangers. They were still there, waving, making begging signs. Catalan approached the edge of the river and threw the bread and cheese. The river was too deep and too swift-running to attempt to cross it at that point. One of the four loaves of bread fell in the water, but the other three and the four pieces of cheese landed safely near Parrado and Canessa. They wolfed down the food.

While Catalan looked on curiously, Parrado took a lipstick from his pocket and printed, in effect, an SOS on a piece of paper. He wrapped the paper in a stone and threw it across the river to Catalan. Catalan read the message, but he wanted more information. He put a pencil in the paper, wrapped it around the same stone and threw it back to Parrado. Parrado then wrote the following:

"I came from a plane that fell in the mountain. I am Uruguayan. We have been walking for ten days. I have an injured friend. In the plane are 14 people, some injured. They have nothing to eat and they can't leave the place. We can't walk further. Where are we? Please, can't you help us?"

Parrado wrapped his note around the rock and threw it back to Catalan. Catalan read it, nodded to Parrado that he understood,

Parrado and Canessa's route from the crash site to the meeting with cattleman Sergio Catalan. Note the relative closeness of the Hotel Termas—in the opposite direction from their route.

then made a signal that he would return. Catalan rode down his side of the river about a half a mile until he saw a friend, Armando Serda, on the same side of the river as Parrado and Canessa. Catalan wrote out a note to Serda telling him to rescue the boys while he, Catalan, went to Puente Negro for help. Catalan wrapped the note around a rock and threw it across the river to Serda. Serda read it and nodded that he understood.

Armando Serda mounted his horse and rode upstream to the place where Parrado and Canessa were waiting. He saw two young men with long beards in grubby clothes, one of them weak and debilitated. Serda returned to his camp for horses. He helped the boys mount, then led them downstream toward Los Maitenes, the group of mud huts near the juncture of the Azufre and Tinguiririca Rivers belonging to Efrain Millan. When they arrived there, about noon, December 21, Efrain Millan and some cowboys welcomed them, gave them lunch and listened to their strange, unbelievable story.

* * *

On the mountainside, the fourteen survivors were not in good spirits. After the C-47 flew over them on Sunday, December 17, they had expected rescue any moment. Then they heard on the radio that the search had been terminated, that the C-47 was returning to Uruguay and they knew that once again they had not been seen. Parrado and Canessa had been gone ten days: undoubtedly they were lost.

They began making plans for a new expedition. It would include everybody except Roy Harley, who was certain to die any day. The food supply, they calculated, would last until January 15. To give the snow more time to melt, they would wait until the last possible day—January 8. Then, in a do-or-die effort, they would all try to walk out.

CHAPTER TWENTY-ONE

A Bolt of Lightning

Sergio Catalan tucked the note from Parrado into his pocket and set off for Puente Negro, about thirty miles away. By then all doubt was gone. The two boys were certainly from the Uruguayan airplane. But how had sixteen survived in the bitter cold without fire or anything to eat? How had the two climbed for nine days in the Andes without equipment?

The first third of the way to Puente Negro was rugged terrain: a narrow trail along canyon walls. After several hours, Catalan reached a small bridge that crossed the Rio del Azufre. On the other side, there was a dirt road leading east to El Flaco, the summer resort, and west to Puente Negro. At that time of year, there was seldom traffic on the road, but by chance, a government truck engaged in road repair came along. Catalan flagged it down. He explained his mission to the workers. They put Catalan's horse in the truck and drove to Puente Negro.

At about 1:30 that afternoon, Catalan reached the Puente Negro police station where the *Carabiñero* Elino Mira Bustamante was on duty. Catalan told him about the two boys and showed him the note.

Corporal Mira could not believe it. It was impossible! Yet he knew Catalan—a neighbor in Puente Negro—to be a responsible man, the owner of many hundreds of head of cattle, the father of seven children. In the evenings, Catalan loved his wine and sometimes became belligerent, but in the daytime, he was clear-headed and intelligent in spite of the poor clothes he wore.

All the *Carabiñeros* at the police station gathered in the front office talking to Catalan and looking at Parrado's note. The chief decided that another corporal, Guillermo Valdez Avila, should take the note to police headquarters in San Fernando, eleven miles away. Valdez drove to San Fernando in a jeep, arriving about 2:30 p.m. He told the unbelievable story and gave the note to the police captain. The captain, though doubtful, went immediately to the office of the mayor. Nobody in the mayor's office could believe the story. They thought it must be a joke—a tasteless joke.

And yet the mayor and police captain also knew Catalan to be a responsible man, not the type to play jokes. The mayor telephoned Colonel Morel at the Colchagua Regiment. Morel was astonished, disbelieving, amazed by the coincidence that only the evening before—when Catalan first saw the two boys—the artist Vilaró was having dinner in his own home. It was *eerie*.

Colonel Morel, a man of direct and forceful action, ordered a patrol of mountain troops, accompanied by medical specialists, to set off at once for Los Maitaenes. Then he remembered that Vilaró had said he was leaving Chile that very day by commercial jet. Morel telephoned the police at Santiago's Pudahuel International Airport, requesting that they find Vilaró and stop him from leaving the country. If they found him, they were to telephone Morel immediately. After that call, Colonel Morel drove to Puente Negro to conduct his own investigation.

Meanwhile the mayor of San Fernando and the police captain, followed by an ambulance, returned with Corporal Valdez to Puente Negro. The mayor and the captain interrogated Catalan. About that time, Colonel Morel arrived. He also interrogated Catalan and examined Parrado's note. Morel copied down the text of the note, then returned to his office in San Fernando. By that time, the patrol he ordered out had left.

Having satisfied himself that the note was no prank—that there was a strong possibility that the two boys were actually from the Fairchild—at 4:47 p.m. Colonel Morel put through a call to SAR headquarters in Santiago. Morel explained what had happened, then read the text of Parrado's note.

When Major Ivanovic received this word, he reacted like everybody else. Impossible, he thought. A bad joke or, more likely, a mistake. Nonetheless, Ivanovic sounded a Red Alert, notifying the helicopter unit of the Chilean Air Force, Group Ten. He then called CSA headquarters in downtown Santiago. The housekeeper at CSA notified the duty patrol. Three experienced climbers, Claudio Lucero, Sergio Diaz, a 47-year-old schoolteacher, and the businessman Osvaldo Villegas, got in the CSA truck and drove to SAR headquarters.

In the meantime, the Chilean pilots Major Garcia and Major Massa, who had planned the initial search for the Fairchild, reported to SAR. They and Ivanovic called the police headquarters in San Fernando and Puente Negro by radio, seeking further information —confirmation that it was all, in fact, true. Nobody they spoke with could supply *official* information, as yet. All they had was the word of Sergio Catalan, a responsible man.

By that time, it was late in the day, too late to launch the helicopters. The air in the Andes would be turbulent. It would be dark by the time the helicopters could get to Los Maitenes for interviews with the two boys. Ivanovic, Garcia, Massa, Lucero, Diaz and Villegas—all good friends and the most experienced of all the Andes rescuers—began making plans for a rescue early the following morning. That is, if the improbable news proved to be true.

As a first step, they sent a radio truck manned by two enlisted men, Francisco Romero and Franco Benfenti, to Puente Negro. When the rescue operations commenced in the morning, they would already be on hand to help coordinate communications between SAR headquarters, the helicopters and the other radio units.

In Puente Negro, the mayor ordered a police expedition to set off for Los Maitenes. It was to bring back something official, a piece of paper at least, declaring the boys were legitimate. The expedition consisted of Corporal Valdez, another *carabiñero* and the medic who drove the ambulance. The medic went ahead, parked his ambulance at the Azufre bridge, then proceeded to Los Maitenes on foot, climbing a difficult and dangerous trail along a canyon wall. The others loaded horses on a truck and set off for the Azufre bridge.

* * *

At Pudahuel International Airport, Páez Vilaró and the pilot Raul Rodriguez checked in at the Argentine Airlines counter. That afternoon, Páez had sent Joaquin Gandarillas a bouquet of flowers for his mother and a note of thanks for his help. He had also acquired a puppy, a Christmas present for his eldest daughter. Páez and Rodriguez passed through customs and International Police and went out to board the aircraft.

As Vilaró was about to climb the boarding ladder, a policeman took him by the arm. What was this? The policeman did not know; he was merely carrying out an order. He led Vilaró and Rodriguez to the airport police office. Vilaró was confused and fearful. He loved Chileans but, as he well knew, the Allende government had assumed the right to arrest anyone on the slightest pretext.

The chief soon put Vilaró at ease. He explained that Colonel Morel of the Colchagua Regiment had called, ordering the detention. Colonel Morel had urgent news of some kind.

The chief called Morel, then gave the phone to Vilaró. Morel said: "My friend, you may go home and spend Christmas with your family, but if you prefer you can return here and come with me to look for the boys."

"What?" Vilaró shouted, excitedly. "What's going on?"

Morel was then more cautious: "Now take it easy. I have some specific information. Two boys came out—I don't know their names yet —and said they were from the Uruguayan plane. I don't know if any of this is true or not." He then read Vilaró the text of the note.

Vilaró listened carefully, restraining an urge to shout for joy. "Shall I wait for you or what?" Morel asked.

"Wait," Vilaró responded. "I'll take a taxi. I'll be there in three hours."

Vilaró and Rodriguez ran to a taxi stand. Vilaró asked a driver if he could take them to San Fernando. The driver begged off. It was nearing Christmas; he had shopping to do. He didn't want to get stuck in San Fernando.

Vilaró explained: "You know the Uruguayan plane that crashed in the Andes? They say it's been found. My son was on the plane."

The driver looked at Vilaró. "Are you that crazy artist who has been looking for his son?"

"Yes. Yes."

"Come on," the driver said. "Get in. I'll take you."

Vilaró hesitated. "There's another problem," he said. "I'm broke. I can't pay you right now."

"Never mind," the driver said. "Get in. How much money do you need? I'll *lend* you money."

Vilaró and Rodriguez climbed into the taxi. The driver sped south toward San Fernando.

* * *

The expedition of *carabiñeros* reached the Azufre bridge at 7:00 p.m. They unloaded the horses and set off at once, going up the dangerous trail. Along the way, they caught up with the medic, who was on foot. They put him on the back of a horse for the last few miles. The party reached Los Maitenes at 10:30 p.m., having traveled the most dangerous leg in complete darkness.

When Corporal Valdez got his first glimpse of the boys, he was somewhat nonplussed. He had expected to find emaciated skeletons, near death. But the two boys were cheerful and appeared to be in fine physical shape, especially Parrado. By that time, they had been resting for almost eleven hours. They had eaten soup, cheese, bread, meat.

Valdez interrogated the boys briefly, took their full names, then wrote out his official report. He did not ask for the names of the boys at the fuselage: Parrado and Canessa were not certain who was still alive. It would be cruel to announce to families someone was still alive when, in fact, he might already be dead. Parrado and Canessa stressed that fourteen had been alive *when they left*.

* * *

While Valdez was compiling his report, the news that two Uruguayan boys had been found in the mountains leaked out, probably by journalists monitoring police radio broadcasts. That evening, Santiago radio and television stations began broadcasting the scanty information. At once it was relayed all over

South America, including, of course, Montevideo, where the stations interrupted regular broadcasts with bulletins. They reported two boys had walked out, and that fourteen others remained alive at the fuselage. There were no names available.

The news hit Montevideo like a bolt of lightning. At first, few could believe it. There had been so many false rumors in the past, so many hopes raised, hopes dashed. In many ways, the news brought on a more trying time for the parents than the initial loss. Many had come to accept the deaths of their sons and had tried to banish the tragedy from their minds. Now it was all back again. Sixteen had been reborn, twenty-nine had died again.

The parents called one another. Some went to the home of a radio ham, Rafael Ponce de Leon, who had been maintaining contact with the ham radio operators in Santiago, Talca and elsewhere in Chile for weeks. Others telephoned the Uruguayan Embassy in Santiago, and spoke with the chargé d'affaires, Cesar Charlone. All had the same questions: Was it true? *Who* were the two who walked out? *Who* were the fourteen on the mountain? As yet, Charlone could not give answers to any of the questions.

When the news broke, Gilberto Regules was at the home of Roberto Francois. Francois's father was one of those who had given up all hope. He prohibited any discussion of the matter in his house. They did not listen to radio or TV. After leaving the Francois home, Regules stopped by the home of another friend in Carrasco. There he heard the news. He would not believe it. He had made a fool of himself when the news of the cross was broadcast, rushing to Montevideo for nothing.

Yet, there was the radio and television going on and on about it. This time there was an air of truth. Surely no one had invented the two boys who appeared in the foothills. Regules swung by the Francois home, relayed the news to Roberto's sister, then went home and informed his father he was going to Chile. His father said no. He should wait for more definite word, such as names. Regules now had some money of his own. He did not need a loan from his father this time, nor, it seemed, permission. He called Iberia Airlines and (like many parents, relatives and friends) made a reservation for Santiago for the following morning. Then he stayed up all night glued to the radio, waiting for hard facts—for names.

In San Rafael, Argentina, two fathers, Roy Harley and Gustavo Nicolich, loyally standing by the C-47 crew, heard the news on the radio. They made plans to leave for Chile at once. The mayor of San Rafael, who had

met them shortly after the emergency landing, lent them his car. They drove to Mendoza. There were no commercial planes for
Santiago and none scheduled to stop. However, there was a cargo plane getting ready
to leave for Santiago with 60,000 pounds of
frozen beef. Harley and Nicolich explained
to the pilot who they were and why they had
to reach Santiago immediately. The pilot took
them on board. There were no seats, but
Harley and Nicolich were happy to sit on
the floor.

* * *

Colonel Morel remained at his office, waiting for Páez Vilaró to arrive from Santiago.
The phone rang constantly. It seemed to
Morel that every journalist in the world was
calling. He had no official information to
give them. All he could do was repeat the
same old story, carefully qualified.

That night at 10:00, three Chileans appeared at his office. They were radio hams,
members of a club from Talca. They had a
radio transmitter set up in a Citroën and
were in touch with the ham Ponce de Leon
in Montevideo, who was besieged with parents and relatives of the Old Christians.

"Colonel," one of the Talca men asked,
"will you please talk to these people?"

Morel manned the radio. For more than

an hour he spoke, one by one, to parents, relatives, friends. His theme was always the same: "Take it easy. It may be true. It may not be true. I have sent a special patrol to find out. The police have sent a special patrol. But it is a long way, rugged country. It will take time. Stand by, please."

At midnight, Vilaró and Rodriguez arrived from Santiago in the taxi. The three men went immediately to the police station in Puente Negro. There, Vilaró examined Parrado's note. He read it with trembling hands, tears welling in his eyes.

"Yes," he said to Morel. "It looks right. Yes, it was written by one of the boys. No doubt about it."

Morel now began to feel the emotion that must have been tearing at Vilaró. Was his son among the living? It seemed to Morel the odds were against it. That was the cruel way of fate. The man who had never given up hope, who had searched relentlessly, was the one bound to lose. Morel did not want Vilaró to lose. He worried how Vilaró would take the shock, or how he, Morel, could possibly break the bad news when it came.

They returned to San Fernando for a late dinner at Morel's home. Vilaró was cheerful, optimistic. His son, he knew, was alive. He had known that all along. The Colonel would see. Hadn't the Dutch seer told them?

After dinner, Morel insisted they sleep for

at least an hour or so. He put Vilaró in a room in the B.O.Q., then lay down on his bed, exhausted.

* * *

All that night, journalists and television and radio reporters streamed in from Santiago. They overran police headquarters in San Fernando, then drove on to Puente Negro. The simple people of Puente Negro (a village of twelve houses) were amazed by this sudden influx, these madmen from the city, who virtually took over the village and never stopped asking questions.

The journalists had a single goal: to find the two boys and get their story. The *carabiñeros* tried to restrain them. The boys were at Los Maitenes, far up in the hills. They would be brought out the following day, probably to San Fernando.

Where was Los Maitenes, the reporters demanded? Far up in the hills, the police repeated. You could only drive so far—to the Azufre bridge—then you would have to go by foot on a dangerous trail. They should not attempt it at night; it would be suicidal. To hell with the risks, the reporters snapped, show us the way.

Corporal Valdez left Los Maitenes with his official report about 11:00 p.m. He rode a horse down the dangerous trail in the dark to the bridge at the Azufre River. There he tied up his horse and got in the ambulance and started down the road for Puente Negro at about 2:00 a.m., December 22. He drove fast, with the ambulance light turned on. Suddenly he was astonished to see a dozen cars, perhaps more, tearing up the road from Puente Negro.

It was the journalists. They saw the ambulance coming from the Azufre bridge toward them and were sure the ambulance must be bringing out the two boys. One reporter slammed on his brakes and spun his car sideways to block the road. Valdez jammed on his brakes, narrowly avoiding a crash. The other cars stopped and a horde of reporters descended on Valdez with television lights and cameras and tape recorders.

The press held Valdez captive for about half an hour, firing questions. Valdez told them nothing—in a dozen polite and different ways. If they wanted official information, he told them, they would have to get it from his superiors. The reporters shouted, threatened, cursed. Then they tore off toward the Azufre bridge, where they abandoned their cars and set off on foot up the dangerous trail.

Valdez reached San Fernando at about 3:00 a.m. He went at once to the office of the mayor. There he found more press and the Uruguayan chargé d'affaires, Charlone. Valdez delivered his official report. It stated that the two boys were Fernando Parrado and Roberto Canessa, Uruguayans from the Fairchild that had crashed on October 13. They had walked for ten days from the wreck, crossing the Andes with primitive equipment. There had been fourteen more survivors when they left. After delivering his report, Corporal Valdez left again for Los Maitenes.

The mayor called Colonel Morel to pass along this first official news. Morel immediately notified Vilaró at the B.O.Q. But Vilaró, who had not gone to bed, already knew from his friends of the Talca Radio Club, who were monitoring the police radio. Vilaró was then relaying the word to Montevideo.

The names of the first two survivors, Parrado and Canessa, were broadcast over the Montevideo radio at 3:30 a.m. Regules heard it, and later Roy Harley and Gustavo Nicolich in the cargo plane.

* * *

On the mountainside, the fourteen left behind spent a fitful night. Before bedding down in the fuselage, Carlos Páez had stated quite emphatically that he had had a vision. Parrado and Canessa, he said, had arrived someplace. They were getting help. Tomorrow, December 22, a helicopter would come to the fuselage to save them. Many believed him.

CHAPTER TWENTY-TWO

A Remarkable Rescue

On the morning of December 22, the fourteen boys on the mountain woke early. Like Carlos Páez, Daniel Fernandez had had a dream. He said: "Parrado and Canessa have arrived. Boys, help is on the way."

They turned on the transistor radio. They heard an announcer talking about a plane crash in the Andes. At first they thought it was another plane that had crashed. Then they heard the names of Parrado and Canessa. They had made it!

They were deliriously happy. They prayed, thanking God. Afterwards, they prepared to leave. Zerbino gathered up all the personal effects of the dead—jewelry, I.D. cards, rings, wrist watches—and put them in a bag. Delgado remembered the red slipper Parrado had given him to bring out. Carlos Páez doused himself with cologne and combed his hair. Then they all sat in the sun by the fuselage, smoking cigars they had found in the tail and saved for this occasion.

* * *

At 6:00 that same morning, the SAR forces gathered at Los Cerrillos Airport in Santiago.

Ivanovic had ordered up three jet-powered Bell helicopters for the mission. The first, H-89, was commanded by Major Carlos Garcia, the senior pilot. His crew: Ramon Canales and Juan Polverelli. The second helicopter, H-91, was commanded by the President's pilot, Jorge Massa. His crew: Juan Ruz and Abel Galvez. A third helicopter, H-90, commanded by Mario Avila, would serve as a support vehicle, bringing extra fuel and supplies.

The three climbers from CSA arrived at 6:30. The teacher Sergio Diaz, the senior climber, was assigned to fly in Garcia's helicopter, along with a female Air Force nurse, Wilma Koch. The other two climbers, Claudio Lucero and Osvaldo Villegas, were assigned to Massa's helicopter. The climbers brought, in addition to the usual climbing gear, tents, a portable stove, sandwiches, soup, cheese and other food.

Ivanovic had not yet received much official information. He knew only that the two boys were at a place near the juncture of the Azufre and Tinguiririca rivers, called Los Maitenes. Neither Garcia nor Massa believed they were from the Uruguayan Fairchild. They did not believe anybody from the plane could still be alive. The three climbers doubted that anyone could have climbed ten days in the Andes without equipment.

Even so, the mission proceeded.

Unfortunately the weather was bad. Thick fog lay all through the valley from Santiago to San Fernando, the first stop. From fifty feet, the pilots could not see the ground. They flew at forty-five feet, following the railroad from Santiago to San Fernando. All three pilots had flown the route countless times. They knew where the tall obstructions were located and maneuvered around them.

While the helicopters were on the way, Colonel Morel, who had slept only an hour, drew up rescue plans with his staff, Uruguayan chargé d'affaires Charlone and Páez Vilaró. Morel had alerted the head of the San Fernando hospital, Dr. Fernando Baquedano, who in turn prepared sixteen rooms, one for each survivor. Morel selected two of his medical men to go on the mission: a doctor, Captain Eduardo Arriagada, and a male nurse, José Bravo.

Morel fretted about the weather. The fog, impossibly thick, was delaying the mission. He maintained continuous telephone contact with Major Ivanovic. Ivanovic reassured him: SAR would fly into hell if necessary.

The three helicopters landed on the soccer field of the Colchagua Regiment at 9:00. Colonel Morel, Charlone, Vilaró and others met them. Vilaró asked Colonel Morel if he could go in a helicopter to the mountain.

Morel said no. The helicopters were already too crowded.

Vilaró was keenly disappointed, yet understanding. He asked the climber Sergio Diaz if he would take a note to his son. Diaz replied, yes, of course, hoping that he would find the son alive. Vilaró then drew a picture of a helicopter on a small piece of paper and wrote: "Hello Carlitos Miguel. As you know, I have never lost faith. Here I send you a helicopter as a Christmas present. Mother is arriving in San Fernando. Love and kisses." Vilaró signed it "El Viejo" (the old man).

The Army contingent, Morel, Dr. Arriagada, and the nurse Bravo, climbed into the helicopters piloted by Garcia and Massa. The third helicopter remained at San Fernando as backup. Dr. Arriagada brought along a supply of emergency medical supplies, including glucose and high-calorie food. Colonel Morel, the expert on the local terrain, flew in the lead helicopter with Garcia. There were six people in each helicopter. They rose into the thick fog and headed east toward Puente Negro.

*　　*　　*

All this time, there had been a steady procession of people heading for Los Maitenes by land: *carabiñeros*, the Army patrol, and the bolder, more enterprising journalists, television and radio reporters and technicians.

Corporal Valdez, who had carried the official report to the mayor of San Fernando, arrived back at the Azufre bridge that morning in the ambulance. He parked it, untied his horse, and set off again on the long dangerous trail. Along the way he found no less than two dozen journalists, lost or worn out or afraid to follow the trail without a guide. Like a Pied Piper, he rounded them up and led them toward Los Maitenes. He laughed at one, an enormously fat man, who paused from time to time to leap into the river to cool off and wash off the sweat.

One of the journalists headed for Los Maitenes that morning was Miro Popic, a star reporter for the Santiago paper *¡Puro Chile!* The paper supported the Marxist government of Allende, and Popic himself was a dedicated communist. At Puente Negro, he had had the good sense to rent a horse. Compared to most, his journey was relatively comfortable.

Popic was one of the first journalists to reach Los Maitenes. He arrived at about 9:30 or 10:00 a.m. and immediately found Parrado and Canessa. Popic was surprised to find them looking so well. He interviewed them: Parrado and Canessa talked freely about the days on the mountain: the crash, the avalanche, finding the tail, the walk out. Popic took notes. In all his years of reporting, there had never been such a story. It was all like a miracle—the miracle of the Andes.

Afterwards, Popic interviewed Catalan, Millan and the cowboys at Los Maitenes. They told Popic that the boys had stayed up until midnight the evening before, telling them all that had happened on the mountain. Popic asked one of the cowboys what the boys had eaten. The cowboy replied: "They buried those who died in the snow and then they ate them."

Popic was shocked and revolted. Until that moment, the boys had been heroes. Now he was confused. Were they heroes or savages?

When Corporal Valdez arrived at Los Maitenes, he was concerned about the weather —the fog. It seemed impossible to him that a helicopter could fly to Los Maitenes. Undoubtedly the rescue of the other fourteen had been canceled pending better weather. He decided to take Parrado and Canessa out on horseback. While the television cameras whirred and photographers scurried around clicking pictures, the *carabiñeros* loaded the two boys on the backs of horses and set off for the Azufre bridge.

* * *

Garcia and Massa had seldom encountered such fog. They flew low, following the road from San Fernando to Puente Negro, Colonel Morel giving directions. East of Puente Negro, Morel told Garcia to turn right and follow the river. They crept up the river into a canyon, flying low. Off to the right, Morel noticed a road where no road should be. They had taken a wrong turn. They were lost.

Garcia (with Massa following) turned around and retraced his flight. They saw a house and landed. Colonel Morel asked the name of the river. It was the Claro, not the Tinguiririca. They continued on through the fog, found the Tinguiririca River, then turned right. Just beyond the Azufre bridge, where the terrain became very rugged, Garcia made the decision to stop the mission until the fog cleared. Anything less was suicidal. They set down in a clearing by the river at 10:10 a.m.

A few moments later Garcia and Diaz saw a movement across the river. It was Corporal Valdez and the other *carabiñeros* taking Parrado and Canessa to Puente Negro. They shouted, but could not be heard over the noise of the river. Corporal Valdez saw them and wrote a note on his handkerchief: "The two boys are here. They know where the wreck is." Then he wrapped his handkerchief over a stone and threw it across the river to Garcia. After reading the note, Garcia realized they had reached Los Maitenes, but had landed on the wrong side of the river. Garcia wrote out a message on the handkerchief: "Thanks. We will continue to Los Maitenes." He wrapped the handkerchief around a stone and threw it back to Valdez.

The two helicopters took off, crossed the river and landed in a field at Los Maitenes. Valdez turned around and returned to Los Maitenes with Parrado and Canessa. When Colonel Morel deplaned, he was swamped by journalists who believed the Fairchild was close by and that the police and soldiers were deliberately concealing the location. Morel, losing patience, told the journalists to go away and leave everybody alone.

After the helicopters landed, Dr. Arriagada examined Parrado and Canessa. He was amazed. Except for cracked lips and conjunctivitis—eye inflammation—and weight loss, they were in fine shape. Parrado was the stronger of the two.

After the examination Dr. Arriagada and Colonel Morel took the boys into one of the helicopters for a private talk. Arriagada said later: "I asked them what they ate on the mountain. Canessa replied, 'Human remains.' He said the food gave out on the eighth day. I then asked them if they had told the reporters they had eaten human flesh. They said no. I told them not to tell the press, otherwise the reporters would destroy them."

After this, the climbers Diaz and Lucero got into the helicopter with Parrado and Canessa. Diaz said later: "The first thing I asked was, what did you eat? Canessa looked at me and said that he was a medical student. He knew that if they did not have protein, they would all die. He stated that they ate human flesh after the eighth day when they heard the search had been called off and that he, Canessa, was the one who compelled the others to eat. I respected his confession and asked no other questions. I was not shocked. As a climber, I know what it is to suffer from lack of food and water. In the Andes, anything goes."

They waited for the fog to clear. While they waited, Garcia, Massa, Diaz and Lucero huddled with Parrado and Canessa, studying maps to locate the fuselage. However, neither Parrado nor Canessa could find the position on a map. All they knew was the Fairchild altimeter showed 7,000 feet. Garcia then decided that one of the boys would have to come along as a guide. Parrado volunteered.

About 11:30, the fog began to clear. By noon, it was mostly gone. Garcia and Massa conferred. Should they break the rule of the Andes and fly in the afternoon, possibly into severe turbulence? Yes, they decided. They would take the chance.

Then a delicate problem arose. The plan was to shuttle back and forth, bringing the boys out four at a time. There were obviously too many people in the helicopters. Colonel Morel gave orders that the female nurse, Wilma Koch, and one of the climbers should remain behind. Diaz did not like this decision. What if the helicopters could not land at the fuselage? They would need three climbers to bring the boys to the helicopter. It would surely be better to have the third climber than Colonel Morel. Garcia—who had the final say—overrode Colonel Morel. All three climbers would go, Colonel Morel would be left behind. Parrado would go in Garcia's helicopter to show the way.

At about 12:15, the helicopters lifted into the air. Above the last patches of fog, they could see the distant peaks of Tinguiririca and La Paloma, and the dreaded banks of cumulus clouds building. Garcia, following Parrado's instructions, flew up the Azufre River. Within a few moments, the helicopters covered the ground it had taken Parrado and Canessa so many days to travel.

At the headwaters of the Azufre, just north of Tinguiririca, they came to a wall of unnamed mountain peaks. Parrado said: "Just over that wall you will find them." Garcia was doubtful. The "wall" was at least fifteen thousand feet high, almost as high as Tinguiririca. But Parrado insisted. "That was where we fell," he said. "I am positive."

Garcia's altimeter then showed 7,000 feet. He radioed Massa that they would climb to 16,000 feet. He started up in a corkscrew flight pattern. Almost immediately they were hit by violent turbulence. The helicopters "shook and spun like leaves in a high wind."

Both pilots fought hard to keep their machines under control. Massa decided it was too dangerous. He radioed Garcia: "Don't climb. Don't climb." Dr. Arriagada said later: "I have flown in every kind of plane under the worst conditions. But this was the worst turbulence I have ever experienced."

Garcia reached 16,000 feet and turned east. The helicopter cleared the peaks by mere feet. Massa followed, holding his breath. The climber Diaz marveled at the scenery. "It was a beautiful place, new to me," he said later. "I made a mental note that someday I would climb those peaks."

They flew east, crossing the Argentine border. Parrado oriented himself by the colors of the peaks. "There's the black one," he said. "And there's the yellow one. The plane is down there."

Garcia looked down. He could see nothing except a hillside of snow and rocks. "There," Parrado shouted excitedly. "It's down *there*."

Garcia could still see nothing. Even so, he began a descent, corkscrewing down from 16,000 feet into the funnel-shaped valley. Again, the turbulence was violent, spinning the helicopter like a toy. Massa said later: "It was impossible. We shouldn't have been out in those conditions. I lost control and we dropped 2,000 feet straight down. I dropped again and barely managed to catch it at 20 feet from the snow."

When they had descended to 13,000 feet and were about 1,000 feet directly over the fuselage, they saw it. Said Dr. Arriagada: "The white fuselage blended perfectly with the snow. If they had camouflaged it, they couldn't have done a better job. It was almost impossible to see."

Sergio Diaz buckled a safety belt and opened a door of the helicopter and leaned out. He could see the fourteen boys below standing by the broken fuselage waving. Diaz gave them a thumbs-up signal. Seconds later, when Garcia passed thirty feet over the fuselage, he threw them a bag of bread and made signs for the boys to eat.

Garcia and Massa circled, studying the slope. It was too steep and windy to attempt a normal landing. The wind would surely blow the helicopters over. They would have to keep the rotors going, holding one ski on the hillside for balance. The climbers would have to jump out and help the boys on board.

Garcia made another slow pass over the fuselage fighting the wind which gusted to 50 knots. Then he shouted to Diaz: "Jump!"

Diaz unbuckled his safety belt and leaped from the helicopter. At that moment, it was about twenty feet from the snow. Diaz sailed through the air and crunched into the snow, sinking waist deep. When the helicopter passed over him again, a mechanic tossed out Diaz's equipment. It landed close—too close for comfort. Diaz picked it up and started walking toward the fuselage. It was 12:45—thirty minutes from takeoff.

"By that time," he recalled later, "the boys were running toward me and shouting. They engulfed me with their arms, almost smothering me. They were happy faces, tears of joy. It was profoundly moving."

Diaz remembered the note he carried from Vilaró. He hoped his son was among the living. He shouted over the roar of the helicopters for Carlos Páez Rodriguez. Later he said: "A good-looking boy, very well-built and in excellent shape stepped forward. I embraced him and gave him the note. He read the note and then he shouted to the other boys, again and again: 'Didn't I tell you the old man was not going to let us down?'"

Diaz now turned to the difficult task of preparing for the rescue. He watched as Garcia settled the helicopter on the side of the slope, the uphill ski touching, the downhill ski high in the air. Some of the boys started running toward the helicopter, but one shouted to Diaz: "Help me. I can't walk."

It was José Luis Inciarte, who had suffered from the lumps on his legs. Diaz picked him up and put him over his shoulder. Then —to his horror—he saw that the boys were running to the uphill side of the helicopter. The rotor was almost touching the snow.

Diaz was certain that some of the boys would be beheaded.

Diaz dropped Inciarte and ran to head them off. He made a signal by drawing one finger over his throat to indicate the danger. Then he pointed to the downhill side, getting over the point that they would have to enter there. He picked up Inciarte again and led the boys, single file, toward the helicopter. He stumbled along carrying Inciarte, with no help from the boys, growing light-headed from the exertion.

When he reached the helicopter, Diaz lifted Inciarte to the side door. Dr. Arriagada and the mechanic grabbed him and pulled him inside. Then Diaz helped up Alvaro Mangino, who was still limping from his broken leg.

In the helicopter, Garcia was worried. It was almost impossible to keep the helicopter level. He ordered Dr. Arriagada to remain in the helicopter. The plan had been for him to get out and administer medicine to the boys who would have to wait for the return trips of the helicopters, but there was no time for that now. Garcia believed that if they didn't take off immediately, the helicopter would be blown into the snow.

Meanwhile Major Massa descended, placing a ski on the uphill slope for balance. The climbers Claudio Lucero and Osvaldo Villegas jumped into the snow. The strongest of the remaining twelve boys ran toward them, shouting and crying. Massa signaled that he could only take two but four jumped in—Carlos Páez, Eduardo Strauch, Antonio Vizintín and Daniel Fernandez.

Worried about this extra weight, Massa turned to the male nurse, José Bravo, and shouted: "Jump!" Bravo, in shirtsleeves, leaped from the helicopter into the snow.

Garcia and Massa gunned their engines and lifted from the ground. Both helicopters were caught in severe crosswinds and turbulence. The helicopters shook violently. The boys were terrified. They clung to one another, shaking with fear. With all the weight he carried, Massa had difficulty gaining altitude. Luckily, he was wafted up by a strong air current. "The Andes does not give up her victims easily," he said later.

In Garcia's helicopter Inciarte and Mangino embraced Parrado, thanking him, stroking his face and beard. When the helicopter began to shake, all three boys were frightened. Mangino asked Dr. Arriagada if it would be a long ride. The doctor assured him it would be brief. Then Inciarte asked the same question. "It was a terrible ride," Dr. Arriagada said later. "Worse than the trip in. All three boys were certain they were going to be killed. I was so busy trying to calm them down I didn't have time to worry myself. I just had one thought: wouldn't it be ironic if the rescuers crashed and had to be rescued?"

There was no crash. In remarkable feats of flying, Garcia and Massa brazened out the turbulence, crossed Tinguiririca and set down on the grass at Los Maitenes. Colonel Morel was there to greet them. When he saw Carlos Páez, his heart swelled with joy. Remarkably, Carlos recalled having met Colonel Morel during his visit to Uruguay in 1971.

The boys embraced Roberto Canessa as they had embraced Parrado. They were delirious with joy. One picked a flower and stared at it. Another fell to his knees, touched the grass and exclaimed about the beauty of green. Others embraced everybody they could find, shaking hands, repeating again and again: "Gracias . . . gracias . . . gracias. . . ."

Garcia and Massa held a conference. They decided there could be no more trips to the mountains that day. It was too dangerous. They would return in the morning when there was less chance of turbulence. The eight boys on the mountain were in good hands. There were three climbers with much equipment and food, plus the male nurse, José Bravo. Garcia radioed Ivanovic his decision. It was accepted without question.

Meanwhile Dr. Arriagada gave each of the six new survivors a quick physical examination. Inciarte was the weakest and most seriously ill. All had cracked lips, conjunctivitis and scurvy—from lack of vitamin C. Some had abscesses on their legs and fungus. Dr. Arriagada gave them chocolate and biscuits and peach marmalade. With each bite, they shouted for joy. He cautioned them not to speak to the reporters about what they had eaten on the mountain.

After the physical examination the boys talked briefly with the journalists. Miro Popic, and others who knew the truth, asked them what they had eaten. The boys fabricated glibly. They said they had bought enormous quantities of chocolate, cheese, meat and wine in Mendoza. When that ran out, they ate lichens, herbs and roots.

Following the press conference, Colonel Morel led the eight survivors back to the helicopters. A few were afraid to get back in the machines, but Morel assured them that it would only be a very brief flight to San Fernando where they were to go to a hospital. The helicopters lifted off, following the Tinguiririca River toward Puente Negro. Within minutes, they reached the Colchagua Regiment soccer field and settled slowly to earth near the ambulances.

There were three fathers waiting: Vilaró, Roy Harley and Gustavo Nicolich, who had come down from Santiago by taxi. The boys burst from the helicopter, Carlos Páez in the lead. He ran to his father. They embraced, tears streaming. Then they pounded one another with their fists. Vilaró swept an arm toward the ambulances and nurses and said: "You see, we have planned a fine party for you."

Some of the boys spoke with Roy Harley and Gustavo Nicolich. Yes, Roy was alive—alive but very weak. Thank God, Harley cried. Gustavo Nicolich? No. Unfortunately, he had died in the avalanche. Tears welled in Nicolich's eyes. He turned away and walked across the soccer field alone.

Colonel Morel, Garcia, Massa, Cesar Charlone, the helicopter crewmen and the nurses and ambulance drivers—indeed, all who saw this scene—were overwhelmed. Few could hold back tears.

*　*　*

All that afternoon, cars streamed down from Santiago to San Fernando, carrying parents, friends and relatives of the boys. In one of the first cars was Madelon Rodriguez, the mother of Carlos Páez, a woman friend, and Gilberto Regules. As they approached San Fernando, they heard the news of the rescue on the radio. Then the announcer began reading the names of the sixteen survivors, obtained from the six who were rescued that day. Madelon Rodriguez could not bear to listen, to learn this way whether her son was dead or alive. She turned off the radio.

In San Fernando, they drove to the Regimental headquarters. Vilaró was standing there, waiting. When Regules saw him, his heart stopped. It seemed to Regules that he looked terribly sad, a sign that Carlos was not among the living. Regules cringed; he did not want to witness this scene. But when Vilaró saw Regules he beamed and ran to the car. Then he saw Madelon in the back seat. He cried: "Madelon, I have a present for you! Carlito. He is here in San Fernando. He is well."

Madelon trembled with joy and thanksgiving. Vilaró embraced her through the window. Then he lifted her from the car to the sidewalk, where they clung tightly, for a long time. "It's a miracle," Madelon sobbed. "A real miracle."

Vilaró gave Regules the names of the survivors, the eight in San Fernando, the eight still on the mountain. Moments later, the father of Eduardo Strauch arrived. When he saw Regules he said: "Is my son alive?"

Regules replied: "Yes, sir. He is here."

Strauch did not believe him. "You lie," he said.

"No, sir," Regules insisted. "He is here. He is well."

The other cars arrived one by one, bringing Seler Parrado, Dr. and Mrs. Canessa, Mrs. Nicolich, Mrs. Harley, Mr. Echavarren, Mr. Inciarte, Mr. Shaw, Mr. and Mrs. Zerbino, others. For each family, it was a time of intense joy or despair—more despair than joy. When Mr. Shaw received the news that his son had died in the crash, he held together just long enough to say: "I have lost one son, but I have gained sixteen others." Then he broke down.

Some families did not leave Montevideo. If the news were bad, they wanted to hear it in their own homes, surrounded by relatives and friends. The parents of the medical student who wrote poetry, Fernando Vazquez, received the news on the radio. Later his mother, who had convinced herself he must be among the living, said: "We sat there— my husband, my daughter, Fernando's fiancée—in the grip of indescribable tension while they read off the names of the sixteen. I kept count on my fingers. Then it was over. There was no Fernando. It was ghastly. For us, Fernando died not once but twice. In October and again in December."

It was the same in many other homes.

CHAPTER TWENTY-THREE

Re-entry

When the first eight survivors reached the hospital in San Fernando, the director, Dr. Fernando Baquedano, was prepared in every respect to treat them for cachexia—an absolute state of starvation. He expected the boys to look like the survivors of a Nazi concentration camp. Instead he received eight boys in relatively good health. Only one, Inciarte, could be classed as "less than normal." Dr. Baquedano and his staff were baffled—until the Army doctor, Captain Arriagada, set them straight.

When the boys had been settled in individual rooms at the hospital, they asked to see a priest. Father Andres Rojas, who was at the hospital chapel preparing for Mass, visited each of the boys alone in their rooms. He heard their confessions. What bothered them most was that they had eaten their friends to survive. Father Rojas explained to each boy that this was not a sin in the eyes of the Catholic Church. The souls of their friends had departed from the bodies at death, he said. They had every right to eat human flesh to keep themselves alive.

Father Rojas made these statements on his own and without hesitation. His superior, Father Humberto Sepúlveda, pastor of the main San Fernando Catholic Church, said later: "All priests are qualified to absolve any sin, except in a few special cases. This was not a special case, not even a sin. He had no need to check with higher authority."

Father Rojas was impressed by the piety of the boys. Father Sepúlveda said: "Their faith on the mountain was a pillar of strength, an inspiration to all Catholics everywhere. They prayed constantly, putting their fate in the hands of God. Every day they said the rosary in the morning and the evening. One of the boys—Carlos Páez—had a rosary made of wood. When he showed it to Father Rojas, the wooden beads were worn down so small they were almost useless."

After making their confessions to Father Rojas, each of the boys received communion in his room.

Later in the day, the parents began descending on the hospital. Dr. Baquedano, wishing to avoid an immediate confrontation between the boys and the parents of those who had died (and thus any emotional discussions of who was eaten and who was not), established a rule that only immediate relatives could see the boys.

There was at least one minor violation of

the rule. Páez Vilaró smuggled Gilberto Regules into his son's room. The two boys stood face to face.

"Hello, Tota," Páez said jokingly. It was a feminine form of Regules' nickname, Tito.

"Hello, Memo," Regules said. "What do you say?"

The two boys embraced. They cried. Then afterwards they talked for a long while. Páez told him how by a miracle "the Gang" had survived the crash. But then Diego Storm and Gustavo Nicolich had been killed in the avalanche, and later Rafael Echavarren, having survived so long and so bravely, died of gangrene. Regules had lost many friends. Half "the Gang" had been wiped out. Of the sixteen survivors, only five were rugby players: Canessa, Parrado, Zerbino, Vizintín and Harley. Ten members of the team—all close friends—had died.

Regules spent hours in the hospital, talking with Parrado, Canessa, Vizintín. During that night, he heard all that had happened on the mountain. When he learned they had eaten his friends to survive, Regules said nothing. Later he said: "They all ate. Some ate more than others, but they all ate."

* * *

After the helicopter left the mountain with the first load of survivors, Sergio Diaz, the senior climber, was astonished to find the male nurse, José Bravo, standing in the snow in his shirtsleeves and street shoes. Diaz went to him.

"What are *you* doing here?" he asked.

"Major Massa told me to jump," Bravo replied. "I followed orders and jumped."

The other two climbers, Claudio Lucero and Osvaldo Villegas, joined them, dragging the bags of equipment. Diaz gave Bravo a fur-lined parka and a pair of boots. Moments later, the wind rose to fifty knots. It blew the equipment, the seats of the airplane hither and yon. Diaz worried about the helicopters, then the eight survivors. It was clear to him the helicopters would not return that afternoon. It was too dangerous. They would have to spend the night on the mountain. The other eight survivors would be disappointed, perhaps severely depressed.

Diaz picked up the bag of bread and sandwiches and took it to the boys and explained the situation—the turbulence. He handed out sandwiches like a Santa Claus. Lucero brought over a tin of butter. The boys scooped it out with their fingers and spread it on their lips and faces. They were disappointed to have to spend another night on the mountain. One or two cried.

While they were eating the sandwiches, Diaz set up the portable stove to melt snow for drinking water. In five minutes he had a jarful. One of the boys said: "Look at that!

He does in five minutes what it took us a whole day to do."

The other climbers and Bravo went off from the group to set up a tent and make a camp. Diaz melted more snow and made some instant soup, enriched with two fresh eggs. He said to them: "Look, *botijas,* lunch will be ready soon."

The boys were surprised to hear themselves called *botijas*—an exclusively Uruguayan expression for "boys"—by a Chilean mountain climber. Lucero explained that his eldest daughter was married to a Uruguayan. He had visited them in Uruguay.

"What a coincidence!" one of the boys said.

"I'll tell you an even greater coincidence," Diaz said. "In Santiago, I live on Uruguay Street. And not only that: my mother, who lives in another section of Santiago, also lives on a street called Uruguay."

There was something more. While in Uruguay, Diaz had bought a salt shaker that was peculiarly Uruguayan. He took it from his bag and showed it to the boys. They recognized it. Some had identical shakers at home.

Later Diaz said: "My purpose was to put the boys at ease, make them feel at home. Some of them were angry they had been left behind and would have to spend another night in the plane. Some were anxiety-ridden. Besides, they had not seen an outsider for seventy days. I believed it was important to treat them as kindly as possible and make their re-entry into civilization as painless as possible. I wanted them to know they had a friend."

Diaz poured the soup into two plastic glasses. The boys sipped and passed the glasses around. While they sipped, Diaz sliced some salami that his wife had given him. After that, Diaz melted more snow and gave them coffee.

"Delicious," a boy said. "Really delicious. And what fast service!"

The medical student Zerbino drew him aside. They walked toward the fuselage. Later Diaz said: "It was then, for the first time, that I saw the cruel reality of survival. There were remains of human bodies all around the fuselage. I did not show surprise or express indignation. I believed that for the psychological sake of the boys, the less said, the less made of it, the better it would be for them."

They went inside the fuselage. Diaz was sickened by the odor of old unwashed clothing and the pilot's body, which was still trapped in the cockpit. He did not want to see more just then. They returned to the group. There was one cigar left in the box. Zerbino offered it to Diaz.

"I don't smoke," Diaz said, "but I will keep it for a souvenir."

Returning the favor, Diaz ripped his CSA emblem from his parka and gave it to Zerbino. "He was wearing the pilot's hat," Diaz said. "He stuck my emblem in the hat."

Roy Harley, reduced to skin and bones and barely able to get around, had a bad reaction to the food. He told Diaz he believed he had diarrhea. But he couldn't move, couldn't make it to the latrine. Diaz had to lift him from the ground and help him.

By that time it was 6:00 p.m. The sun went down behind the peaks and the temperature fell rapidly. It was time to take shelter. By then, Lucero and Villegas had set up the tent about fifty feet from the fuselage. Diaz had planned to sleep in the tent with his companions, but Roy Harley and Javier Methol, who was emotionally upset, pleaded with Diaz to sleep in the fuselage. Diaz thought of the revolting smell, but nevertheless he agreed to go with the boys.

"Again," he said, "it was a matter of keeping up their spirits. Harley and Methol did not want me to leave their side."

Lucero, Villegas and Bravo, who had been stamping snow and laying out pieces of aluminum to make crude heliports, came to the fuselage to help Diaz prepare dinner for the boys. Lucero did the cooking. It was more soup (instant Russian soup which Lucero had obtained on a "nonpolitical" climbing trip to that country), canned beans, more bread. The climbers sang songs and cracked jokes. At about 10:30, the others returned to the tent, leaving Diaz alone with the boys, who gave him a poncho-blanket. Diaz lay down beside Harley in the forward end of the cabin, body athwartships, like the others.

"The boys had a lot of things they wanted to get off their minds," Diaz said later. "Principally, they were concerned about how the fathers of the boys they had eaten would react, and how society would react. I assumed the role of father, teacher and psychologist, because I knew that what I said would be very important for their spirits and the re-entry. I told them, candidly, that it was going to be very difficult for them. Because of the terrible circumstances fate had placed them in, all their lives would change significantly, perhaps drastically. I told them they could best compensate the families of the eaten by being humble. That is, adopting a lifestyle of humility."

To pass the time—no one could sleep— Diaz recited poetry and then, like a teacher, forced the boys to memorize a poem, *The White Rose*, by the Cuban José Martí:

> I'll grow a white rose
> In June as in January
> For the sincere friend
> Who gives his hand sincerely.

And for the cruel,
Those who would stab my heart,
I cultivate not weeds nor thorns,
But a white rose.

At midnight Diaz said: "Well, boys, what do you know! It's my birthday. I am 48 years old."

The boys were astonished and happy. They sang happy birthday. And so the night passed.

At dawn Diaz got up and went down to the tent, where his companions were having breakfast. Diaz ate with them, then took the portable stove back toward the fuselage to prepare breakfast for the boys. On the way he set the stove in the snow and walked around the fuselage, taking mental notes. Near the left rear of the fuselage, he found the bodies of three women: Eugenia and Susana Parrado and Liliana Methol. They had not been touched. Near the right rear of the fuselage, he found the bodies of four boys that had not been touched. All seven bodies were covered with snow. He did not check the body of Ferradas in the cockpit; the nose of the plane was then too high off the snow. One of the boys had told him that Ferradas' body had no head.

Zerbino came out and they talked. Diaz thought they had better make a drawing showing the location and names of all the bodies. Zerbino identified the three women and the four boys at the fuselage. (Echavarren and Turcatti were two of the four.) He told Diaz there were five more bodies uphill at the crash site: the navigator, Martinez; the steward, Ramirez; Guido Magri; Gaston Costemalle; Alejo Hounié. None of these bodies had been touched. There was one at the tail, Juan Carlos Menendez, also untouched. In all, thre were thirteen intact bodies, or fourteen, if the headless Ferradas were counted.

"The other fifteen were mostly just bones," Diaz said later.

Diaz returned to the plane to prepare breakfast. He made coffee and fried bread in a frying pan. The boys laughed when Diaz burned his hand and spat a Chilean curse-word: "¡Rechucha!"

After breakfast Diaz helped the other climbers finish the helipad, then watched the skies. It was a beautiful day with little or no wind, no clouds. This time, it would be easy for SAR. There would be no turbulence. If three helicopters came, they could remove all twelve of them in one operation: four men to each helicopter.

At about 9:15 that morning, December 23, Diaz saw the helicopters returning. There were three of them, but only two—H-89, piloted by Garcia, and H-91, piloted by Massa—landed. The third helicopter, H-90, piloted by Mario Avila, was hovering overhead at 16,000 feet, maintaining radio contact with SAR headquarters, a precaution should both Garcia and Massa fail to get off the ground.

The three climbers and José Bravo helped the eight survivors into the helicopters. They were: Roberto Francois, Roy Harley, Alfredo Delgado, José Algorta, Adolfo Strauch, Gustavo Zerbino (who turned over the bag of personal effects to SAR), Javier Methol and Ramon Sabella.

Garcia and Massa flew directly to Los Maitenes. There they unloaded the boys and returned to the fuselage an hour later. An Air Force doctor, Captain Eduardo Sanchez, flew with Garcia. When they reached the fuselage, Massa circled overhead while Garcia made his third landing there. Captain Sanchez got out for about five minutes to survey the site and look at the bodies.

Ordinarily the climbers and SAR would have continued working until all bodies had been recovered and returned to San Fernando or Santiago. Afterwards they would have been inspected by a judge, who would have issued a burial permit to the relatives. However, there were legal problems involved in this case. Human beings had been eaten. There were only fourteen out of 29 bodies to return, one headless. Besides that, all these people had died in Argentina, not Chile. Because of all these factors, they decided they should leave the bodies and remains at the site until higher authority could decide what should be done.

The three climbers and José Bravo threw the gear into Garcia's helicopter and climbed aboard, followed by Dr. Sanchez. Garcia gunned the motor and lifted off, climbing in a corkscrew pattern to 16,000 feet.

Massa, meanwhile, had been flying close to the peak where the Fairchild hit. He conducted an aerial inspection, locating the wings, the two engines and the landing gear. He saw the five bodies uphill. "They seemed to be sitting in a circle, heads bowed," he said later, "as though participating in some strange rite." Massa made a crude map of the debris and bodies and photographed all with still and movie cameras.

After that, Garcia and Massa returned to Los Maitenes. From there the three helicopters carrying the eight survivors, the three climbers and José Bravo went on to the Colchagua Regiment in San Fernando.

*   *   *

That morning, more and more parents, relatives and friends of the living and dead arrived at the San Fernando hospital, followed by dozens of journalists and television and radio reporters. Colonel Morel, Dr. Baquedano and the Uruguayan chargé d'affaires, Cesar Charlone, were overwhelmed. Where would all these people stay? The one hotel in San Fernando, a small, second-class establishment, was already overflowing. Colonel Morel, who had spent most of the previous evening caring for the families, inviting many to his home, had no room at the regimental headquarters.

They reached the only reasonable solution: the second group of survivors would be taken directly by helicopter to the main hospital in Santiago. The first group would leave San Fernando that day by car and ambulance. In Santiago, the parents, relatives and journalists could find ample hotel accommodations. The officials of San Fernando, most of whom had not slept in several days, could get some rest.

That morning, the journalists at the hospital tried every gambit of the trade to get interviews with the boys. But the police and soldiers, under orders from superiors, would permit no contact. One journalist, Marcelo Mendieta from the Buenos Aires paper *La Nación*, was more persistent than the others. He and a Buenos Aires television reporter, Carlos Campolongo, got by the police barricade in the lobby and made their way into an inner courtyard where they found Parrado and Canessa sitting in a room.

Mendieta, formerly a police reporter and then a special correspondent who covered

big stories for *La Nación,* had by chance
come from Buenos Aires on the same plane
with Dr. Canessa. Dr. Canessa had told Mendieta that he expected to find his son Roberto
and Parrado and the others suffering from
cachexia. Thus, when Mendieta got his first
glimpse of the two boys, he was surprised
and curious. "My antenna went up right
away," Mendieta said later.

Mendieta tried to coax the boys outside
into the courtyard, so that Campolongo could
have light to photograph them. They were
hesitant—until Campolongo told them he
had attended the Christian Brothers School
in Buenos Aires and had played rugby. With
that, the ice was broken.

Parrado stood for a moment in silence.
Then, as Mendieta recalled, he said: "How
beautiful it is to hear the birds singing."

Mendieta said to Parrado: "You have
broken all records for survival in the Andes.
What are your rules?"

"The first rule," Parrado replied, "is to have
faith in God. Without Him, nothing is important."

Parrado hesitated. Mendieta prodded.

"The second rule is you must have faith in
yourself, a strong will to live."

"And the third?" Mendieta asked.

"The third is that you must accept whole-
heartedly the laws and rules, however strange
or unusual they may be, set up by the new

community which you have created for survival."

Mendieta wondered, at that, what did he mean?

When the other journalists realized that Mendieta and Campolongo had scored a beat, they broke through the police barricades into the courtyard. They were followed by relatives and friends of the survivors. The other six survivors came from their rooms and suddenly—and unintentionally—a wild press conference had got underway.

"It was unbelievable," Mendieta said later. "People pushing and shouting. Cameras going. Guys running out of tape cassettes for their recorders and grabbing someone else's. Everybody was talking at once: the survivors, mothers, fathers, brothers, sisters, sweethearts."

One reporter from Buenos Aires put the question directly: "What did you eat at 12,-000 feet? How did you survive?"

The boys spoke of herbs, roots, lichens. Some mentioned flies and bees. A father shouted that they had eaten birds. But none of the reporters was satisfied. The boys seemed evasive. Said Mendieta: "They kept looking at one another as though they were monitoring each other's conversation. Then they all started talking in this vague, mystical way about God, faith, religion. Carlos Páez said that when the wind blew hard they became fearful and prayed three Our Fathers. When they did that, he said, the wind seemed to stop. One of them raised his arms in a messianic way and said: 'Only faith can save the world.'"

One of the Chilean reporters rejoined: "How can you say that when the world is the way it is and nobody believes anything anymore?"

Carlos Páez broke in arrogantly: "That's what *you* think."

Parrado told a Buenos Aires reporter: "We have gone through moments of great anguish in the midst of total desolation. You find yourself in a situation like that and all that counts is to go on living. For this reason, we ask you not to keep asking how we survived. We have seen friends or relatives die with tears in our eyes and have been completely impotent in the face of the white silence of the Andes. We thought that for all of us, the world would end there. . . ."

After an hour, a doctor appeared and broke off the conference. Mendieta and most of the other journalists who had been present left knowing that they had not been told the whole truth. Many were disenchanted with the boys, not because of what they might have done on the mountain to survive, but because they had not been candid. Others resented the continual emphasis on God and religion.

Later that morning the eight boys went to the hospital chapel for Mass, to which the public had been invited. A bishop was present, along with Fathers Sepúlveda and Rojas and two other priests. At the Homily, the bishop invited the boys to thank God for their survival and to pray for the dead and the families of the dead. One by one, the boys stood and prayed. Those who were in wheelchairs, remained seated and said their prayers. The families joined in the prayers. The boys received communion for the second time in 24 hours.

Following Mass, the boys prepared to check out of the hospital and go to Santiago. Inciarte and Mangino went in ambulances. The other six went in private cars with their families and friends.

* * *

The three helicopters bearing the second eight survivors and the climbers landed at the Colchagua Regiment soccer field at about noon. Colonel Morel, Charlone, Páez Vilaró and some other parents were on hand to greet the boys. Páez sneaked Mendieta and another reporter, Julio Arganaraz, by the guards, then raced to the helicopter to embrace the second group. Mendieta, following Páez, heard Adolfo Strauch say to Vilaró: "You see, *El Viejo*, we do not look so bad, now do we?"

The helicopter paused at the soccer field only long enough to refuel. They took off again at 12:55, flying directly to Santiago and landing on the helipad on the roof of the main hospital. Roy Harley was removed on a stretcher and sent immediately to intensive care. Roberto Francois had his right eye bandaged: he had suffered from snow blindness. Javier Methol was weak, mentally upset and suffering from malnutrition. Some had sores on their legs. All had cracked lips and inflamed eyes.

Those who were able had showers. Then a nurse called them together for lunch. They had steak, tomatoes and a cake in honor of all those who had had birthdays on the mountain—Nune Turcatti, Carlos Páez, Roberto Francois, Fernando Parrado, Javier Methol, and Alfredo Delgado. In the afternoon, the other eight arrived from San Fernando by car. There was a wild and happy reunion. Still later, all those who were able went to Mass again, and the second group, who had confessed to a priest, had communion.

* * *

That day the journalists returned to Santiago to write their stories. One of these was Miro Popic, star reporter for *¡Puro Chile!*, who had been told by the cowboys at Los Maitenes the day before that the boys had eaten human flesh to survive. Popic was morally torn. Like most Chileans, he loved the Uruguayans. If he wrote the truth, he knew, it would not only cast the boys in a bad light but also damage relations between Chile and Uruguay.

After a long struggle with his conscience and discussions with his editors, Popic decided that he was a journalist first, a diplomat second. However, he resorted to a small compromise: instead of headlining cannibalism, he headlined survival and buried the sting deep inside his story. His story—the first published account of cannibalism in the Andes—appeared that day, December 23rd.

Later that night Marcelo Mendieta went to a news service in Santiago, borrowed a desk and wrote his story for *La Nación*. He filed a straight story with no mention of cannibalism. There were other reporters there from Argentina and Uruguay. About midnight a man came into the office bringing what he claimed to be an official report of the CSA. He gave it to Mendieta.

Mendieta read hurriedly, then began making brief extracts which he recalled later: "When —— got to the ground, he almost stepped on the arm of a woman. He knew it was a woman's arm because the nails were painted. He could see that the palm of the hand was missing as well as part of the forearm . . . —— looked around hi min the snow and could see other parts of the human body scattered around . . . parts of skulls, legs, arms. When he was headed for the fuselage —— stopped and picked up what remained of a man's head. It was a skull. 'Who was he?' —— asked [a] young man. The young man replied: 'It was the pilot of the plane. We ate his brains but we respected his body. It is still trapped in the cabin. . . .'"

Mendieta, a tough reporter who had dealt with many lurid stories in his twenty-year career, had been half-expecting this news, but still he was shocked. After the man left with the alleged official report, he sat at his desk for a moment, shaking his massive head. Then he shoved the extracts in his pocket and went out to walk the streets. He had planned a big dinner, but he no longer felt like eating. Like Popic and other reporters, he wrestled with his conscience: tear up the extracts or publish them?

His debate was more or less academic. By then, Popic and other reporters were filing stories of cannibalism to papers in Peru, Venezuela and Argentina. Soon it was moving on news tickers the world over. In the days following, the cannibalism story was published in every country in the world, except Uruguay. The editors in Montevideo, who work under government censorship, considered the story too shocking, too macabre, too embarrassing for a small nation that already had its share of problems.

"We had to think of the families of the dead," a Uruguayan reporter said later. "And besides that, Uruguayans simply do not like to read anything unpleasant."

CHAPTER TWENTY-FOUR

An Intimate Communion

On Christmas Eve, the boys left the hospital and moved to the Sheraton San Cristobal Hotel on a hillside overlooking Santiago. The parents gave them a gay party and dinner. On Christmas Day, they attended a special Mass at Catholic University. Everywhere they were greeted as heroes; young girls overran the hotel seeking autographs.

José Luis Inciarte, who made a remarkably swift recovery, said: "This is the best Christmas I ever had. I feel like a huge baby that has just been born from a pregnancy that lasted two months."

On the day after Christmas there was a sour note in the chorus of adulation. Miro Popic of *¡Puro Chile!* obtained a copy of what was alleged to be the official report of the CSA. Under large headlines, he published excerpts similar to the extracts Mendieta had made. Another paper, *La Segundo*, did likewise. In the days following, two other papers, *El Mercurio* and *La Tercera de La Hora*, published shocking photographs of a human leg in the snow by the Fairchild fuselage. The foot was covered with a shoe but there was no flesh above the ankle.

The stories touched off an official uproar. The CSA denied that it had leaked its official report to the press. SAR, which had been dragged into the papers, took pains to point out that its official report dealt only with aircraft rescue operations, not with what may have been found at the fuselage. The Allende government intruded, asking Santiago editors to stop publishing alleged reports of cannibalism. The newspapers, in turn, attacked one another for sensationalism or for deliberately fomenting trouble between Chile and Uruguay. Some papers that had published sensational stories or photographs defended themselves editorially, claiming that they had merely printed the truth for truth's sake.

The boys and the parents were dismayed and enraged. Fernando Parrado told a reporter: "We ate what food there was on the airplane, then survived. There are things we will never talk about. They are not important. They should not be talked about." The mother of Roberto Francois told a journalist that the reports of cannibalism were a lie and that they were besmirching "a miracle from heaven." José Pedro Algorta was of a different mind. "From the first moment," he told a reporter, "we should have said directly what we were forced to do during the critical situations we faced in the mountains. I believe we should now talk about it naturally and with dignity." Cesar Charlone went on radio and confirmed the reports, hoping to end the speculation and rumors. Charlone, in turn, was denounced by a Uruguayan politician as "unhuman."

Ugly rumors spread. One had it that one of the boys (later killed in the avalanche) became so enraged at the pilot that he killed him with his pistol. The Chilean Air Force launched an official investigation, taking statements from the boys, the CSA climbers and the men of SAR who had participated in the rescue. However, the investigation got nowhere. Whatever had happened on the mountain had happened in Argentine territory; the Chilean government did not have legal authority to conduct an investigation. The Argentine government displayed no interest in conducting an investigation. The Uruguayan Air Force began an investigation into the cause of the crash, but it had no authority to probe matters that might have happened on Argentine soil after the crash. For these reasons, no thorough interrogation of the boys was ever made by any official body—Chilean, Argentine or Uruguayan.

The disclosures of cannibalism had one curious and unexpected side-effect: it turned the boys into hot literary properties. They were hounded by journalists and television crews who offered large sums of money for exclusive interviews. Parrado gave several. Carlos Páez sold a roll of color film for $500. Vizintín and others made separate deals. Páez Vilaró and his son gave an exclusive interview to a Santiago magazine, *Paulo*. Young Carlos said he intended to write a book. His father, Vilaró, said *he* would write a book. Parrado said *he* would write a book.

The overriding public relations problem then was what to say and how to say it when they returned to Uruguay, where the rumors of cannibalism were rampant but where no newspaper had yet published a line about it. The Uruguayan reporters were certain to raise questions. The boys could not very well deny it. Ultimately the families of those who had died would find out from one source or another. Some might give angry statements to the Uruguayan press or bring legal action.

The fathers of the boys took charge of this delicate problem. They decided that it should be handled at one carefully staged press conference with heavy religious overtones. The boys and the families would return to Montevideo on a chartered jet. From the airport they would go directly to Stella Maris School and hold their press conference in the gymnasium. Each of the boys would speak briefly on a different aspect of the tragedy. One boy would concede anthropophagy. Two or three fathers would speak in support of the boys. Afterwards they would have another Mass and communion, with the highest-ranking church officials they could find.

The fathers, working with Chilean authorities, made one other important decision. They would make no attempt to bring down the bodies or parts of bodies from the mountain for burial in Uruguay. They would bury all the remains in a common grave on the mountain. That way, nobody in Uruguay would ever know exactly which bodies had been eaten and which had been left untouched. The boys could tell each parent that his son "had been respected."

One father—Ricardo Echavarren, father of Rafael Echavarren—was opposed. The boys had conveyed Rafael's last will to him and Rafael's request that he not be abandoned in the Andes. The father was determined to carry out his son's last request. Dr. Helios Valeta, father of Carlos Valeta, who sank in the snow after the crash and died, tried to talk Echavarren out of his position. He said: "As a doctor, I have seen many terrible things. But I do not believe I could stand to go up there." However, Echavarren held to his position. They could do as they pleased; he was determined to return his son's body to Uruguay.

Echavarren requested official help in Chile to bring down the body. Everybody refused. He went to see one of the cowboys in the mountains to ask if he would lead an expedition to the wreck. He refused. Echavarren then decided that sometime in the future—after the snow melted—he would go himself to the grave and get his son's body.

The Uruguayan chargé d'affaires, Cesar Charlone, who helped the fathers with these decisions, left in advance of the others to firm up arrangements in Montevideo. When he landed at Carrasco Airport, where reporters were waiting to interview him, he had a rude jolt: A woman—it turned out to be Estela Ferreira, the widowed mother of Marcelo Perez, the team captain who died in the avalanche—rushed at Charlone shouting insults. She said: "You return as a hero, but in Chile you were miserable." She was angry, she told reporters, because Charlone had not tried hard enough to persuade SAR to continue the original search for the plane and other reasons. One may have been that Charlone had confirmed the reports of cannibalism.

Charlone was amazed and confused. The Uruguayan reporters ran after him, shouting questions. Charlone begged off: first he had to consult with the Foreign Minister. The reporters were furious and joined Estela Ferreira in hurling insults. One shouted: "You talk in Chile. Why don't you talk here?"

Charlone hurried to his car. In the confusion he got in the wrong one. When he found the right one, he hurried off to the Foreign Ministry. Later he talked with reporters stating: "When the boys come home you will find out how much I helped them."

* * *

The chartered jet—an LAN-Chile Boeing 727—was made ready at Pudahuel Airport on the afternoon of December 28. Only ten boys were booked for the flight. Roberto Francois, Alvaro Mangino and Daniel Fernandez had already gone ahead. Fernando Parrado was unable to go. His father, grieving the loss of his wife and daughter, had gone into seclusion at the Chilean beach resort, Piña del Mar. Parrado remained by his side. José Pedro Algorta went directly to Buenos Aires to be with his family. Roy Harley, who had been recovering nicely, had a setback and had to return to the hospital.

The plane was scheduled to take off at 4:00 p.m. Nine of the boys arrived on time with their families and friends. They were dressed informally, with sport shirts, slacks, jackets. The tenth boy, Antonio Vizintín, was late. He had been giving an exclusive television interview. When he finally buckled his seat belt, the hostesses—part of the special "antipanic" crew—gave the usual spiel about what to do in an emergency, displaying oxygen masks and pointing to the emergency exits. The boys laughed merrily.

When the jet taxied for takeoff, some of the boys became anxious and nervous. Most sat on aisle seats so they couldn't see out the windows. José Inciarte, sitting in a center seat between his brother and girlfriend, crossed himself repeatedly. Some prayed aloud. At 5:15, the plane lifted from the runway.

It was late afternoon. There was severe turbulence in Juncal Pass, the direct route from Santiago to Mendoza. The pilot plotted the reverse course that Lagurara and Ferradas had planned for the Fairchild: Santiago, Curico, Planchon Pass (where the turbulence was reported to be lighter), Malargue, Mendoza. They reached Curico within a few minutes, then turned east to cross the Andes. One or two boys looked out the windows, but most did not. Roberto Canessa told a reporter: "I am a little nervous . . . I am thinking about the Andes below. They are terrible and lovely. They have a cruel fascination."

At 6:30, the jet crossed the Rio de la Plata and entered Uruguayan skies. Ramon Sabella looked down and said: "Uruguay is nice—no mountains." Eighteen minutes later, as the plane descended for a landing at Carrasco Airport, the boys sang the Uruguayan national anthem. Few in the cabin could hold back tears.

Thousands of people had gathered at Carrasco to greet them. José Inciarte was first to deplane. He wore sunglasses and raised his arms in greeting, like an astronaut returning from the moon. It was drizzling; nobody seemed to notice. The crowd cheered. The wife of the President of Uruguay, Josefina Herran, the most important of the official greeters, moved toward the ramp to welcome the boys home, followed by Daniel Juan, president of the Old Christians. Police kept the throngs of press and the curious at a distance.

After the landing, Javier Methol split off from the group. He went directly to his home, where relatives had been caring for his four children since October 12. The emotional strain of the reunion with his children was overwhelming. Later Methol had to be placed again under the care of a doctor.

The other nine boys and relatives walked to two big new buses, waving, smiling, shouting to friends in the crowd. At about 7:15, the buses left the airport.

When the nine arrived at the Stella Maris gymnasium, there were about 500 people jammed inside the building: relatives, friends, families of the dead, members of the Old Christians wearing red armbands and acting as ushers, priests, the Christian Brothers from the school, journalists and television and radio reporters. The small stage of the gym had been set up for the meeting. There was a long table, a podium with microphones, a flag of Uruguay, a flag of Chile and the symbol of the Old Christians' rugby team. The Bishop of Montevideo sat on the stage. Television cameras were zeroed in on the podium.

The boys went to the stage and raised their arms in greeting, making a victory sign with their fingers. The crowd cheered and applauded. Then, as Daniel Juan approached the microphone, it became so quiet, one reporter wrote, "you could hear a fly flying."

The conference, Juan explained, would be conducted in two parts. First the boys and some fathers would speak. Secondly, the boys would answer questions from the press.

After Juan's introduction, the boys came to the podium one by one to talk briefly, and somewhat vaguely, about their experiences. Antonio Vizintín spoke first, then Zerbino, Canessa, Adolfo and Eduardo Strauch, Inciarte, Carlos Páez. Ramon Sabella broke off his talk midway, overcome by emotion.

The boys and fathers had chosen the 25-year-old law student, Alfredo Delgado, to be the spokesman on anthropophagy. Delgado was not a Stella Maris graduate and not a rugby player and therefore conveyed an air of impartiality. He stood at the podium and spoke quietly and confidently: "When we found we were out of food, we thought of Jesus and how He had divided His body and blood among the apostles during the Last Supper. And at this moment, He was telling us what to do—to take His body and blood.

Then we would be born again. And that was a very intimate communion between all of us. And that helped us to survive. This is for us a very intimate, intimate, intimate thing. And we don't want it made light of. In foreign countries we talked about this very seriously. And here in our own country we tell you this very seriously. And you have to remember the valor of the boys who died. . . ."

The crowd applauded and cheered for two minutes.

Afterwards two fathers, Jorge Zerbino and Páez Vilaró, spoke briefly. Zerbino, a lawyer, defended the boys, painting them not as a barbaric tribe where the fittest survived, but rather as pious monks, trapped by circumstances. He reminded the audience that the boys had tried everything to save the lives of the injured, including Canessa's operation to remove the rod from Platero's stomach. "They were like a community in which the weakest were the most protected," Zerbino said. "When there was not much food, the sick and injured ate first. . . . When one has faith in God, when one wants to live, anything goes. I salute the families of all those who died. . . ." Zerbino concluded his talk with unqualified praise for Cesar Charlone, who received the news at home on his radio gratefully.

Páez Vilaró rose and said: "The boys have suffered the Calvary of Christ. Today, they are sixteen Christs, an example for those of you who have lost faith in youth. All 45 are here today, with pure minds and pure bodies. . . . Join me in an Our Father."

The prayer concluded the first part of the press conference. There was no second part. Not a single reporter asked a question.

The ceremony was concluded with Mass. The Bishop of Montevideo presided, assisted by ten other priests. For his sermon, the Bishop chose the story of the miracle of Lazarus rising from the dead. Bringing the full weight of the Catholic Church in support of the boys, the Bishop read a message from Cardinal Antonio Maria Barbirei, congratulating the sixteen for their faith, solidarity and love. The boys, parents, relatives and friends had communion and sang hymns.

After the ceremony the reporters mingled with the parents of the living and the dead. They found that Dr. Helios Valeta, whose son was among those eaten, was not bitter. On the contrary, he said: "Thank God there were 45 so that sixteen could live." Later, in an interview with Ignacio Suarez, he amplified: "I knew they had to eat the flesh of the other boys. There was no other choice. I wondered who had decided this and how they had done it. I wondered if my son had helped them survive. Now I know they did eat him. I accept this, as a father and as a doctor. In spite of my grief I believe my son's body had a more beautiful destiny than just decaying in the earth . . . Everyday millions of people save their lives through blood transfusions. This blood is also human tissue. Nobody is horrified by this. I accept what the boys did. They were in extreme circumstances.

"All this has made me reflect deeply about the miracle of life. I bring many people into the world every day routinely. But in the past days, I have stopped to think about this. A mother with a newborn son asked me what I should name him. I said: 'Name him Carlos Alberto, the name of my son.'"

Not all the families of the dead were so forgiving.

CHAPTER TWENTY-FIVE

Fulfilling a Last Request

While the survivors scattered to Uruguayan beach resorts and ranches to be with their families and friends, Chilean officials in Santiago wrestled with the legal problems raised by the death of 29 people and made arrangements for the mass burial. It was complicated every step of the way by the fact that the crash had occurred on Argentine soil, in a place that was inaccessible and dangerous.

First there was the question of the death certificates. Who would issue them? The Chileans? Argentines? How could they get a judge to the scene of the accident to view the bodies as required by law? Would it be necessary to reassemble the dismembered bodies in order to make a positive identification?

After days of meetings and discussion with the Argentines, it was finally decided that the usual rules could not be followed. No judge went to the site. The death certificates were issued by the mayor of San Fernando and registered at the San Fernando courthouse. They were signed by the Army doctor, Eduardo Arriagada, who had flown with

Major Garcia on the first rescue mission but had never seen the bodies. He gave the date of death for all 29 as October 13, the date of the crash, even though he knew from the survivors the approximate date of death of each.

Second was the question of the mass burial. Who would carry it out? And what about Ricardo Echavarren's request that his son's body be brought down? Should it be honored? Was there not a *legal* obligation to honor it? What if Echavarren had been eaten?

After many more days of discussion, it was decided that the Chileans would conduct the burial. The original plan of a common grave for all 29 people would be adhered to. Echavarren was denied permission to bring his son's body down. No relatives of the dead would be permitted to attend the burial. It was too dangerous and too horrible.

The Chilean government assigned the task of carrying out the burial to SAR and the CSA. Captain Mario Jiminez of SAR was named to head the expedition. The senior climbers Sergio Diaz and Claudio Lucero headed the sizable CSA contingent, which included a mountain-climbing priest from San Fernando, Ivan Caviedes, who would conduct the Requiem Mass. The Uruguayans were represented by the Operations Officer of the transport group to which the Fairchild had been assigned, Captain Enrique Crossa. He was also preparing an official report on the crash for the Uruguayan Air Force.

Ricardo Echavarren was less than pleased by these decisions. In secret he continued making plans to bring down his son's body —mass burial or not. He met privately with Sergio Diaz. He gave Diaz pictures of his son and asked Diaz to attach a tube to the boy's body containing Rafael's First Communion Certificate. He also asked that the body be buried last, on top of the others. The First Communion Certificate would enable Echavarren to identify the body quickly and without disturbing the others. Somewhat reluctantly, Sergio Diaz agreed.

* * *

The burial expedition geared up to leave on the morning of January 18. On the preceding day Major Garcia flew over the site in a DC-6 to check conditions. They looked bad. It was summer and the snow was melting fast and crashing down the hill in avalanches. Clearly, the burial operation would be dangerous.

The next day SAR, staging from the summer resort El Flaco, lifted the expedition to the site by helicopter. In all there were twelve men. The two helicopters made two flights each, carrying three men and equipment. By 10:00 a.m., all had been landed safely. By 11:00, they had set up a camp of three tents about a hundred yards from the fuselage. The first casualty was the SAR radio operator, Fredy Bernales Jara. He forgot his sunglasses and was blinded by the glare of the sun on the snow.

The twelve men divided tasks. Some picked up the remains of the bodies that had been eaten and put them in large plastic bags. Others inserted the intact bodies into bags. Sergio Diaz found Rafael Echavarren's body, put it in a plastic bag and tied the tube containing his First Communion Certificate on the outside. The toughest job was that of removing the headless body of the pilot, Ferradas, from the cockpit. It took all twelve men to pry the instrument panel back and free the body, an appalling task since the body was decomposing.

Four men, including the priest, Ivan Caviedes, volunteered to dig the grave. Caviedes picked a snow-free site overlooking a valley about a quarter of a mile east of the fuselage. The ground was rocky and hard. The men had to use pickaxes. At that altitude, each swing of the pick required tremendous effort.

The four gravediggers were almost killed. At 2:15, while they were hacking away, a huge avalanche rumbled down the slope toward them. Someone saw it coming and shouted. The men scattered out of the way.

Five minutes later, another avalanche came boiling down. The second brought a portion of the Fairchild's wing with it and two of the five bodies that had been uphill near the point of the crash. The wing came to rest about a hundred yards from the fuselage.

Sergio Diaz was concerned. The work was far more dangerous than they had believed it would be. They had planned to stay four or five days, but Diaz sent out an urgent radio message: they would wind up the work in one more day. He posted an "avalanche watch" to warn the workers.

The Uruguayan pilot, Captain Crossa, tried to gather some technical information that would help him solve the mystery of the crash. It was a futile undertaking. The boys had hacked out the VOR, ADF, the radio, the altimeter and other instruments that might have provided clues. They had burned or destroyed all the paperwork. Crossa could not find a single item of value to his research.

Crossa then undertook to destroy the fuselage, and with it the memories of what had transpired there. He piled all the old filthy clothing and poncho-blankets inside the cabin and doused the debris with gasoline brought for this purpose. He set off the gasoline with a match. The flames gutted the fuselage, but did not destroy it. It remained, a charred skeleton.

On the following morning, January 19, the

expedition set to work at 7:30. Father Caviedes and his group continued digging the grave, a shallow hole twenty feet by twenty feet. Others dragged the bags of bodies and pieces of bodies from the fuselage to the grave. One expedition went to the tail to retrieve the body down there. Another climbed to the top of the mountain and brought down the last three bodies. This expedition found one of the engines uphill poised directly— and dangerously—above the camp.

They worked as fast as possible, ever fearful of avalanches. There was good reason for the fear. Between 2:10 and 3:50 p.m., nineteen avalanches rumbled down the hillside. The avalanche watch shouted warnings for each, enabling the men to scurry out of the way. One avalanche passed within fifty yards of the camp. Another brought down the engine.

On the following morning, January 20, at 7:00, Father Caviedes went to the grave and held the burial service. At its conclusion, he scattered a handful of Uruguayan dirt over the rocks and planted a small iron cross in the rocks forming the grave. The Chileans in San Fernando who made the cross had adorned it with two inscriptions. On one side it said: "The world to their Uruguayan brothers—1972." On the other it said: "Nearer My God to Thee."

A few hours later, the SAR helicopters returned and lifted the men and their gear off the mountain. In the days following, Cesar Charlone held a press conference to thank all Chileans for their help in the search, rescue and burial of the dead. With that conference, he said, the unhappy event was now closed, finished forever.

* * *

He was wrong. It was not yet finished. Ricardo Echavarren, dedicated to carrying out his son's last request, provided the final curtain.

For weeks after the burial ceremony, Echavarren sought legal permission to unearth Rafael's body and return it to Uruguay. When this effort came to naught, he decided that he would go there and bring it down himself. He enlisted the help of the architect Gustavo Nicolich, a good friend and one of those who had flown in the Uruguayan C-47 and thus knew the area and the problems that would be encountered in an expedition.

In March Echavarren and Nicolich left for Mendoza. Echavarren had a friend in that city, Ricardo Franchetti, a farmer. Franchetti introduced Echavarren to the owner of a local newspaper. Franchetti and the newspaper owner helped Echavarren and Nicolich plan the expedition. The newspaper owner volunteered two reporters, Francisco Fernandez Quintana and Juan Antonio Dominguez, who were excellent climbers. In San Rafael, Nicolich got help from his friend the mayor, who had lent him the car to drive to Mendoza the night Parrado and Canessa were found.

The expedition, consisting of Echavarren, Nicolich and the two newspapermen, set off from San Rafael, March 20 at 6:00 a.m. They drove west into the Andes to a place where they had arranged to meet two mountain men, Rene Lima and Antonio Ayala. They left the car there and continued by horseback, with Lima and Ayala serving as guides. They had three mules also: two to carry supplies and one to carry Rafael's body. They climbed in a westerly direction for three or four hours, stopping for the night at Tres Lagunas.

At 6:00 a.m. the following morning, March 21, they set off again toward the west. Soon they came to the Hotel Termas in the shadows of giant Mount Sosneado. It was about five miles as the crow flies from the hotel to the wreck. Neither Nicolich nor Echavarren spoke of it, but both had the same thought: if the boys had tried to walk out to the east instead of the west they would have reached the hotel in a day and a half at the most, even in the deepest snow. The hotel was closed in October, but it was stocked with firewood and canned food. They could have subsisted very well there, obtained their bearings from the maps in the hotel and walked out to civilization following the Atuel River downhill to the east. Had this been done before the avalanche of October 29, both their sons would have survived.

They forded the Atuel River, then followed the Las Lagrimas River west. They picked flowers to put on the grave. At 9:00 a.m. they spotted the tail section through binoculars. An hour later they reached it. They remained there for an hour, looking around, taking pictures. They found a hood with wire drawstrings and mittens that the boys had made. They also found the radio antenna and the note left there by Parrado, Canessa, Vizintín and Harley on December 7. They also found many suitcases, including the one that Nicolich had given his son. The combination lock was broken.

At 11:00 they continued uphill toward the fuselage and the grave. It was a steep and difficult journey. After an hour they had to dismount. Nicolich and Echavarren, panting from the high altitude, lagged behind and had to stop to rest every 50 yards. The newspapermen and mountain men continued on.

About noon Nicolich and Echavarren reached the burned-out fuselage. They poked around the mass of debris, took photographs and stared at the hulk where both their sons had died. It all seemed incredible:

the crash, the avalanche, the survival, the deaths. They appreciated then what those 70 days must have been like.

Afterwards they went to the grave. They lifted off the rocks and found the plastic bag containing the body of Rafael Echavarren, identified by the First Communion Certificate in the tube. To be doubly certain, Echavarren opened the bag and looked at the face of the body. It was Rafael. Nicolich did not try to find the body of his son.

They put the flowers on the grave, then placed the body on a makeshift sled made from the back of one of the aircraft seats and lowered it down the slope to one of the three mules. They tied it on the mule, then began the return trip, stopping again at the tail. Echavarren and Nicolich invited the mountain men to take some of the clothes that were in the suitcases, but both men refused. They insisted, stating that as parents, they were authorized to give away the clothing as gifts. With that, the men helped themselves.

They pressed on, retracing their steps to the Hotel Termas. They arrived at about 11:30 p.m., having traveled the last three hours in darkness. They met an unexpected reception at the hotel: police. The police arrested them for graverobbing, sending them to San Rafael. There Echavarren and Nicolich explained that they had not "robbed a grave" but rather had merely removed the body of Echavarren's son in order that it could receive a proper burial in Uruguay. The newspapermen defended them, pleading with the police to be reasonable. But the police were adamant. They refused to release either Echavarren or Nicolich until a Federal judge intervened. The judge released them on condition that Echavarren report to officials in Malargue the following day. In the meantime, the police kept Rafael's body.

When Echavarren reported to the police in Malargue, they fingerprinted him and threatened to put him in jail. But Nicolich, the journalists and the mayor of San Rafael brought pressure to bear and Echavarren was released. Afterwards he went to Buenos Aires and began the legal proceedings that would enable him to bring Rafael to his final resting place in Uruguay. Until that was finally done, Rafael's body remained in niche number 105 in the San Rafael Cemetery.

CHAPTER TWENTY-SIX

"What Would You Have Done?"

So ended the most incredible survival story of modern times. All who were touched by it, however remotely, would never forget it. They remembered every detail of where they were and what they were doing and thinking during each phase of it, the way middle-aged Americans remember the moment the attack on Pearl Harbor was announced.

Gilberto Regules was one of those. Months afterwards he could recall all about the night before the plane was to leave Montevideo, the complicated arrangements for getting a ride to the airport, leaving the wake-up call with UTE—everything except going back to sleep that morning, the sleep that may have saved his life.

And he was still angry about it. About missing the plane. His friends and teammates who survived—Carlos Páez, Antonio Vizintín and others—had one-upped him. They had had an experience in the Andes that set them apart, transformed them in a period of 70 days from boys to men. Regules was jealous—and curious about himself.

"I wish I had been on that plane," he said. "I'd like to know how I would have reacted.

Would I have caved-in or would I have been a leader? Would I have had the will to live and done what was necessary to survive, no matter how drastic? Wouldn't you be curious? What would *you* have done?"

PASSENGER LIST

Survivors

1. Roberto Jorge Canessa Urta—19
2. Javier Alfredo Methol Abal—36
   Celebrated his 37th birthday on December 11.
3. Adolfo Luis Strauch Urioste—24
4. Eduardo José Strauch Urioste—25
5. Roy Alex Harley Sanchez—20
6. José Luis Nicolás Inciarte Vazquez—24
7. Roberto Fernando Jorge Francois Alvarez—20
   Celebrated his 21st birthday November 23.
8. Fernando Seler Parrado Dolgay—22
   Celebrated his 23rd birthday on December 9.
9. Daniel Fernandez Strauch—26
10. José Pedro Jacinto María Algorta Durán—21
11. Alvaro Mangino Schmid—19
12. Antonio Jose Vizintín Brandi—19
13. Carlos Miguel Páez Rodriguez—18
    Celebrated his 19th birthday on October 31.
14. Ramón Mario Sabella Barreiro—21
15. Gustavo Zerbino Stajano—19
16. Alfredo Daniel Delgado Salaberri—24
    Celebrated his 25th birthday on November 1.

The Dead

1. Felipe Horacio Maquirriain Ibarburu—22
2. Gustavo Diego Nicolich Arocena—20
3. Fernando Vázquez Nebel—20
4. Gaston Costemalle Jardi—23
5. Arturo Eduardo Nogueira Paullier—21
6. Numa Turcatti Pesquera—24
   Celebrated his 25th birthday October 30.
7. Marcelo Pérez Ferreira—25
8. Jorge Alejo Hounie Sere—20
9. Julio Martínez-Lamas Caubarrere—24
10. Guido Magri Gelsi—23
11. Daniel Agustine Maspons Rosso—20
12. Carlos Alberto Valeta Vallendor—18
13. Francisco Domingo Abal Guerault—21
14. Rafael Echavarren Vázquez—22
15. Daniel Gonzalo Shaw Urioste—24
16. Juan Carlos Menéndez Vilaseca—22
17. Enrique Platero Riet—22
18. Francisco Nicola Brusco—40
19. Esther Horta Pérez de Nicola—40
20. Eugenia Dolgay Diedug de Parrado—50
21. Susana Elena Alicia Parrado Dolgay—20
22. Graziela Obdulia Augusto Gumila de Mariani—42
23. Liliana Beatriz Navarro Petraglia de Methol—34
24. Diego Storm Cornah—20
25. Colonel Julio Cesar Ferradas Benitez—39 (Pilot)

26. Lt. Colonel Dante Hector Lagurara Guiado—41 (Co-pilot)
27. Lt. Ramon Martínez Rezende—30 (Navigator)
28. Carlos Roque Gonzales—24 (Mechanic)
29. Ovidio Joaquin Ramírez Barreto—26 (Steward)

THE MORNING OF THE
MAGICIANS 50p

Louis Pauwels and Jacques Bergier

"Two theories were current in Nazi Germany:
the theory of the *frozen world*, and the theory
of the *hollow Earth*.
"These constitute two explanations of the
world and humanity which link up with
tradition: they even affected some of
Hitler's military decisions, influenced the
course of the war and doubtless contributed
to the final catastrophe. It was through his
enslavement to these theories, and especially
the notion of the sacrificial deluge, that
Hitler wished to condemn the entire German
race to annihilation."

The incredible yet highly regarded theories of
the frozen world and the hollow Earth have
never before been expounded in this country.
They are two amongst many such theories,
including for example man's evolution
towards some kind of mutant superman,
that have remained secret and hidden in
Britain while gaining strong popular support
elsewhere. Now a new awareness is growing
in our minds, and much of our new
understanding we owe to this famous book
and its two intrepid authors. Their
interpretation of human affairs, very
different from that put forward by ordinary
historians and commentators on day-to-day
events, is much nearer to the unexpressed
instincts of the people.

THE FAMILY   40p
Leslie Waller

Truly great novels about the Mafia are few
and far between. *The Family* is not only
the most recent but one of the very, very best.
The *New York Times* called it "a jumbo
entertainment, full of everything" and drew
attention to the book's shattering
combination of big business, violence, raw
sex, protest and comment on the richest
society in the history of the world. It is a
dramatic and engrossing story that exposes a
new breed of gangster less concerned with
strong-arm tactics than with financial
manipulation. Woods Palmer, chief executive
of America's biggest banking empire,
becomes the pawn in an operation of a naked
ruthless power that only the Mafia's mighty,
complex machine can wield with such
effectiveness and shameless brutality.

*All these books are available at your local bookshop or newsagent: or can be
ordered direct from the publisher. Just tick the titles you want and fill in
the form below.*

Write to Mayflower Cash Sales Dept., PO Box 11, Falmouth,
Cornwall.
Please send cheque or postal order value of the cover price
plus 7p for postage and packing.

Name ....

Address ....

....